NEED YOU NOW

N. Viktoria

Copyright © 2025 by **N. Viktoria**

All rights reserved. No part of this publication may be reproduced, distributed or transmitted in any form or by any means, without prior written permission.

N. Viktoria/Alphazuriel Publishing
United States

Publisher's Note: This is a work of fiction. Names, characters, places, and incidents are a product of the author's imagination. Locales and public names are sometimes used for atmospheric purposes. Any resemblance to actual people, living or dead, or to businesses, companies, events, institutions, or locales is entirely coincidental.

Cover © 2025 Anchorage

Need You Now/N. Viktoria -- 1st ed.
ISBN 9798265175793

CONTENTS

CHAPTER ONE 1
CHAPTER TWO 47
CHAPTER THREE 91
CHAPTER FOUR 129
CHAPTER FIVE 172
CHAPTER SIX 211
CHAPTER SEVEN 247
CHAPTER EIGHT 279
CHAPTER NINE 337
CHAPTER TEN 377

CHAPTER ONE

Zara Baptiste pressed her back against the research ship's metal wall and tried to stay calm. The morning sun was hot on her dark skin, but inside she felt cold as ice. Something was wrong on this boat. Real wrong.

She'd been living a lie for six months now. Everyone on the *Deep Explorer* thought she was Dr. Zara Baptiste, some smart college professor who wrote articles about old ships for National Geographic magazine. But that was bullshit. The real truth was scary as hell.

She was DEA Agent Zara Baptiste, and she was hunting fifty million dollars worth of stolen diamonds. Blood diamonds from Africa that some dirty federal agent had stolen from evidence lockup six months ago. Diamonds that were now somewhere on the bottom of the Caribbean Sea, waiting for someone to find them.

The boat's engine made a weird coughing sound, then died completely.

"Shit," Zara whispered under her breath, the way her grandmama had taught her never to do in public. But Grandmama wasn't here in international waters with a boat full of men who'd been acting strange for weeks.

Captain Morrison walked over, sweating even though the morning breeze felt nice. "Just some engine trouble, Dr. Baptiste. Nothing to worry about."

Everything to worry about, more like. Zara had grown up in Miami's Little Haiti, and she knew when people were lying. Morrison's eyes kept moving around, never looking straight at her. His hands shook a little when he talked. And two of his crew members were standing too close, like they were ready to grab her if she tried to run.

Her cover was blown. These men knew she wasn't really a professor. The question was what they planned to do about it.

"I'll just take some pictures of the engine room," she said, trying to sound normal and professor-like. "You know, for the magazine article."

"Engine room's off limits right now," Morrison said fast. Too fast.

Not asking. Telling.

Zara's heart started beating harder, but she kept her face calm. Six months of living this lie had taught her how to act. She needed to get below deck and use her emergency radio to call Agent Martinez, her handler back in Miami. Federal protocol said to call for backup when operations went bad.

And this one was going bad real quick.

"How long until we can move again?" she asked, like any normal person would.

"Could be hours," Morrison said. His eyes flicked toward the two crew members, and they started moving to block her path to the stairs.

These were men she'd eaten dinner with for months. Men who'd told her jokes and asked about her fake research. Now they looked like they wanted to hurt her.

The boat suddenly tilted hard to the left, throwing everyone off balance. Water was coming in somewhere. Zara grabbed the railing as the deck slanted under her feet. This wasn't weather - they were sinking.

Someone wanted this boat on the bottom of the ocean, along with everyone on it.

"Fire in the engine room!" a voice shouted from below. Black smoke started pouring out of the hatches, thick and nasty-smelling.

Real emergency or fake setup to kill her? Didn't matter now. The *Deep Explorer* was going down for sure, and Zara needed to survive long enough to report what she'd learned about the diamond operation.

She ran toward her cabin while the crew shouted and ran around the tilting deck. Her emergency kit was hidden behind the bathroom mirror - waterproof bag with backup radio, federal ID, GPS tracker, and the memory card with six months of evidence about who was stealing diamonds from the government.

The boat was leaning worse now, with cold ocean water rushing through the lower decks. Zara grabbed her emergency bag and headed for the life raft area. Her federal training said this was probably a trap, but the water around her ankles was definitely real.

She got to the main deck just as the ship's alarm started screaming. The *Deep Explorer* was dying fast, sinking front-first with water pouring over the front rail. Life rafts were supposed to inflate automatically when they hit the water.

But they weren't inflating. They were sinking like rocks.

Someone had cut the inflation cords.

"Dr. Baptiste!" Morrison yelled, waving at her. "Over here, quickly!"

Like hell. Zara clutched her waterproof bag and jumped over the back rail.

The Caribbean water was cold and salty and way deeper than it looked. But her body remembered every swimming lesson from Miami Beach, every summer afternoon diving for shells with her cousins in Biscayne Bay. Uncle Ronny had been a fisherman, and he'd made sure all his brother's kids could swim like dolphins.

"Ocean gonna test you someday, *ti fi*," he used to say in Creole. "Better be ready when it do."

Today was that test.

Zara dove deep, swimming hard away from the sinking ship. Above her, the research vessel was tilting more and more, air bubbles streaming up through the blue water like silver balloons. Men were shouting from the deck, some jumping overboard, others still trying to get the sabotaged life rafts working.

She surfaced sixty yards away, treading water and watching the *Deep Explorer* die. The back end of the ship rose up out of the water, propeller spinning in the air, then the whole thing slid under the waves with a sound like a giant taking his last breath.

Six months of undercover work, gone. But the memory card in her bag had enough evidence to nail the bastards who were selling conflict diamonds, if she lived long enough to get it back to Miami.

Movement in the water made her look around. Three crew members had made it away from the sinking ship, swimming toward some floating coolers and life jackets. She started swimming toward them to help.

Then she saw Morrison in the water, and he wasn't swimming like someone who was scared. He was swimming straight toward her, and something metal flashed in his right hand.

A diving knife.

Zara turned and swam toward open ocean as fast as she could.

Growing up in Miami had meant more than just casual beach trips. Uncle Ronny had taught all his nieces and nephews how to handle deep water, because the ocean around South Florida could kill you if you didn't respect it. He'd made them swim for hours, teaching them how to float, how to conserve energy, how to survive when the land was too far away to reach.

"Water don't care if you rich or poor, black or white," he used to say. "But if you smart and you strong, you can make it care about keeping you alive."

Time to find out if he was right.

She settled into a long, steady stroke, pacing herself for survival. Nassau was about forty miles away, but she didn't have forty miles in her. The morning sun was getting hotter, and even in October the Caribbean heat would be brutal by afternoon.

Her waterproof bag slowed her down a little but also helped her float. More important, it had the emergency beacon that might save her life. She activated it while treading water, hoping the signal would reach Nassau Coast Guard or any ship close enough to help.

Behind her, Morrison and his guys were spreading out in the water, searching. Looking for her, or looking for other survivors to kill? Either way, distance was her friend.

Zara kept swimming northwest, toward the shipping lanes where cruise ships and cargo boats traveled between islands. Someone had to be monitoring emergency radio frequencies. She just had to stay alive long enough for rescue to arrive.

The sun climbed higher and the water felt warmer against her body. That was dangerous - she was losing body heat even in tropical temperature. Hypothermia could kill her before thirst or exhaustion did.

She'd been swimming for maybe thirty minutes when she heard engines.

Multiple boat engines, getting closer.

Zara stopped swimming and listened, trying to figure out which direction the sound was coming from. Definitely boats, but were they rescue or more trouble?

A white boat appeared on the horizon, heading straight for her. As it got closer, she could see it was a big sport fishing boat, maybe sixty feet long, with Australian flag at the back and serious fishing gear all over the deck. The name painted on the front said *Siren's Call*.

Not Coast Guard, but not Morrison's people either.

She waved both arms over her head and yelled as loud as she could. "Help! Over here!"

The sport fishing boat turned toward her, engines slowing down as it got close. Zara could see four people on deck - three men and a woman, all looking at her in the water. The man driving the boat had light brown hair bleached by sun and the kind of tan that came from years on the ocean.

"Jesus, mate, what happened to you?" he called out in an Australian accent as the boat pulled up next to her. His voice sounded genuinely worried, and he moved with the kind of authority that came from knowing what he was doing on the water.

"Shipwreck," Zara managed, treading water beside the big white hull. "Research vessel went down fast. I think I'm the only one who made it."

Not exactly true, but close enough for now.

Strong hands reached down to pull her up onto the boat. The Australian captain looked like he was in his mid-thirties, with green eyes that didn't miss anything and scars on his palms from handling ropes and fishing equipment. His crew moved like professionals, wrapping her in blankets and checking to make sure she wasn't hurt.

"I'm Captain Ryder MacCallum," he said, kneeling beside her as she caught her breath on the deck. "This is my crew - Miguel, Jin, and Tomás. We picked up your emergency signal about twenty minutes ago."

"Dr. Zara Baptiste," she replied, sticking to her cover story. "Marine archaeology professor. I was on the *Deep Explorer* doing research when she went down."

His eyes got a little narrow. "Marine archaeology, eh? What kind of research?"

"Caribbean shipwrecks," she said, which was sort of true. The diamonds she was hunting had gone down with a merchant ship last year during hurricane season. "Historical trade routes, Spanish colonial period stuff."

"Interesting work." Ryder's voice was neutral, but she saw him look at his crew. "Any idea what made your ship sink?"

Zara hesitated. These people had just saved her life, but her federal training said don't trust anyone until you know whose side they're on. "Engine fire, I think. Everything happened really fast."

Miguel, a compact guy with Mexican features and kind dark eyes, handed her a bottle of water. "Drink slow," he said in accented English. "Saltwater dehydration is dangerous, *mija*."

The Spanish word for "daughter" made her think of home, of her own family in Miami who thought she was still working a desk job for the DEA. She nodded and sipped the water, using the time to study her rescuers.

Professional boat crew, definitely. Their equipment was expensive and well-maintained. The diving gear looked serious - the kind of stuff you'd need for deep-water work. Metal detectors, underwater cameras, archaeological documentation equipment.

Either very dedicated sport fishermen, or something more interesting.

"What's your business out here?" she asked, trying to sound casual.

"Treasure hunting," Ryder said with a small smile. "Legal salvage work, proper permits and everything. We work with museums and historical societies, documenting finds before we bring them up."

Zara's pulse jumped. Treasure hunters in these waters could be anything from legitimate archaeological researchers to black market artifact smugglers. And considering what she'd learned about the diamond trafficking operation, she didn't believe in coincidences.

"Any luck recently?" she asked.

"We're working on something promising," Jin replied. The Korean woman looked to be in her thirties, with smart eyes and the precise movements of someone who worked with technical equipment. "Spanish merchant vessel, went down in last year's hurricane. Records suggest she was carrying valuable cargo."

The pieces clicked in Zara's mind like a lock opening. Spanish merchant vessel. Hurricane last year. Valuable cargo.

The *Caribbean Star*. The ship that had been carrying fifty million dollars in conflict diamonds when she sank in deep water. The same ship whose cargo was scattered across the ocean floor, waiting for someone to find it.

These people were hunting the same treasure she'd been tracking for six months.

"Sounds fascinating," Zara said, keeping her voice academically interested. "I'd love to hear more about your research methods."

"Always happy to talk shop with a fellow maritime archaeologist," Ryder said, but something had changed in his voice. Professional courtesy mixed with careful evaluation. "Why don't we get you some dry clothes and hot food? You've been through hell today."

Jin led her below deck to a small but nice cabin. The *Siren's Call* was clearly designed for long trips - professional navigation equipment, satellite communications, dive preparation areas that could work as research stations too.

"There are clothes in the locker," Jin said, pointing to a narrow closet. "Should be something that fits. Miguel's making soup - you need to get your core temperature back up."

Alone in the cabin, Zara quickly changed into dry jeans and a t-shirt that smelled like sea salt and adventure. Her emergency bag sat on the small desk, waterproof seal intact. The evidence inside could make or break the federal case, but it could also get her killed if these people weren't who they claimed to be.

She turned on her backup communication device and sent an encrypted message to Agent Martinez: "Deep Explorer down. Crew hostile. Rescued by treasure hunters. Will maintain cover and report in 24 hours."

The device confirmed the message went through, then she turned it off and hid it in the bag's secret compartment.

Whatever game was being played out here, she needed more information before showing all her cards.

When she came back to the main deck, the crew was gathered around a chart table, studying ocean maps and historical documents. The kind of research that real treasure hunters would do, or very thorough criminals.

"Feeling better?" Ryder asked, looking up from a detailed chart. "Miguel's soup should help with the shock."

"Much better, thank you." Zara accepted a steaming mug from the Mexican crew member. The soup smelled like seafood and spices, rich and warming. "I can't thank you enough for picking up my beacon."

"Lucky we were in the area," Tomás said. The Brazilian navigator had the weathered look of someone who'd spent decades reading ocean conditions. "These waters can be dangerous for survivors."

"What's your plan now?" Ryder asked, leaning against the helm console. "We can run you into Nassau, get you to the Coast Guard station for debriefing."

Zara sipped the soup and thought about her options. Nassau meant federal contact, proper backup, extraction from the operation. It also meant explaining six months of undercover work to bureaucrats who might not understand how urgent it was to find those diamonds.

And it meant leaving behind the best lead she'd found - a treasure hunting crew that was apparently searching for the same shipwreck that held her target.

"Actually," she said carefully, "I'm wondering if I could stay with you a bit longer. My research was focused on that same Spanish merchant vessel you mentioned. If there's a chance to document the site properly..."

Ryder's green eyes studied her with new interest. "You're talking about joining our operation?"

"Temporarily," Zara said. "I've got maritime archaeology credentials, underwater photography experience, historical research that might help your survey work. My magazine would pay well for exclusive documentation rights."

It wasn't completely a lie. National Geographic would pay well for that kind of access, if Dr. Zara Baptiste were real.

"Interesting proposition," Ryder said, looking at his crew. Miguel nodded slightly, Jin looked thoughtful, and Tomás shrugged like he was willing to be convinced.

"What specific research have you done on the *Caribbean Star*?" Jin asked.

Zara's heart jumped. They knew the ship's name. That confirmed they were hunting the same target, but it didn't tell her whether they knew about the diamonds.

"Cargo manifests from the Spanish archives," she said, drawing on the real historical research that had been part of her cover preparation. "The *Caribbean Star* was carrying more than the official records show. Private cargo, undocumented items that passengers and crew brought aboard."

"Undocumented cargo," Ryder repeated, and something flickered in his expression. "That could make things very interesting."

"My research suggests significant value," Zara continued, walking the line between truth and deception. "Items that would be worth recovering for historical preservation."

"Historical preservation," Miguel said with a slight smile. "Of course."

They knew something. Maybe not the full story, but they knew the *Caribbean Star* had been carrying something more valuable than trade goods and passenger luggage.

"So what do you say?" Zara asked, meeting Ryder's eyes directly. "Partners in maritime archaeology?"

He was quiet for a long moment, studying her with an intensity that made her wonder what he saw. A real researcher with useful skills, or something more complicated?

"We'll give it a try," he finally said. "But understand, Dr. Baptiste - this isn't a university project. The work is dangerous, the conditions are challenging, and we operate by certain rules out here."

"I understand," Zara replied.

She was beginning to think she understood very little about the situation she'd stumbled into. But one thing was clear - these people were her best chance of getting close to those diamonds and completing her mission.

"Excellent," Ryder said, reaching out to shake her hand. His grip was firm and warm, callused from years of boat work. "Welcome aboard the *Siren's Call*."

As the boat changed course and started heading toward open water, Zara stood at the back rail and watched the last pieces of the *Deep Explorer's* debris field disappear behind them. Six months of careful undercover work had ended with sabotage and crew members who might or might not have been trying to kill her.

Now she was on a treasure hunting boat with an Australian captain who made her pulse race every time he looked at her, hunting fifty million dollars in conflict diamonds with people who might be criminals, legitimate businessmen, or something in between.

Her grandmother had always said the ocean would either save you or kill you - it never stayed neutral.

Zara was about to find out which side it had chosen.

As the sun reached its peak and the *Siren's Call* settled into a steady course southwest, she caught pieces of conversation from the wheelhouse. Ryder's voice, low and serious, talking to Jin about equipment preparation and dive schedules.

"...if the cargo manifest is accurate, we're looking at significant recovery value..."

"...authentication will be crucial for the museum partnerships..."

"...those diamonds could change everything..."

Diamonds.

Zara's blood went cold. They weren't just hunting the *Caribbean Star* for historical artifacts or general treasure. They knew about the diamonds specifically.

The question was: were they federal allies, international criminals, or something else entirely?

And more importantly, did Captain Ryder MacCallum realize that his new maritime archaeology partner was a federal agent with a very personal interest in those same diamonds?

The game had just become much more complicated.

But as Zara watched Ryder's competent hands on the wheel and listened to his crew plan their approach to the dive site, she felt something she hadn't experienced in months of undercover work.

Hope.

These people moved like professionals who cared about doing things right. Their equipment was legitimate, their permits were in order, and their research was thorough. If they really were hunting the diamonds to clear someone's name or serve justice rather than profit, they might be exactly the allies she needed.

The afternoon sun was hot on her dark skin as the *Siren's Call* cut through blue Caribbean water toward whatever waited at the *Caribbean Star* coordinates. Behind them, Nassau disappeared into heat shimmer and distance. Ahead lay answers to questions that had consumed six months of her life.

And beside her at the helm stood a man whose green eyes and sun-weathered hands made her think about things that had nothing to do with federal missions or conflict diamonds.

Things that could get them both killed if she wasn't careful.

Things that might be worth the risk.

The *Siren's Call* moved through Caribbean waters like she was born for it, twin diesel engines purring with the kind of reliability that came from proper maintenance and experienced hands. Zara found herself assigned to help Jin with equipment inventory, a task that let her study the boat's capabilities while maintaining her archaeology professor cover.

"These metal detectors are military grade," she observed, running her hands over sophisticated detection equipment that cost more than most people's cars.

"Ryder has connections," Jin replied, checking calibration settings with technical precision. "Former Royal Australian Navy, maritime interdiction operations. He knows where to get the good stuff."

Naval background. That explained the way Ryder moved with unconscious authority and his crew's almost military efficiency. It also raised questions about what kind of maritime interdiction he'd been involved in, and whether those operations had included conflict diamond smuggling.

"What kind of interdiction?" Zara asked casually.

"Drug runners, arms smugglers, people trafficking," Miguel said, joining them at the equipment station. "The kind of work that makes you enemies in some very dangerous places."

"Is that why he left the navy?"

Miguel and Jin exchanged a look, the kind of glance that said they knew more than they were willing to share with someone they'd just met.

"Ask him yourself," Jin finally said. "But maybe wait until you've been aboard longer than six hours."

Fair enough. Trust had to be earned, especially in international waters where federal law enforcement was complicated and backup was hours or days away.

The afternoon sun was getting intense, beating down on the boat's deck with the kind of heat that made everything shimmer. Zara's protective braids were holding up well in the humidity, but she could feel sweat beading on her forehead and between her shoulder blades.

"You handle the heat pretty well," Tomás observed from the helm, where he was taking his turn at the wheel while Ryder studied charts below. "Most people from up north, they wilt like flowers in this sun."

"I'm from Miami," Zara said. "Born and raised in Little Haiti. This weather feels like home."

"Ah, a Caribbean sister," Miguel said with approval. "That explains the swimming. Most people can't survive what you went through this morning."

"Uncle Ronny made sure all us kids could handle the water," Zara replied, letting her Miami accent slide into the words naturally. "Said the ocean don't care about your problems, but if you respect it and know what you're doing, it might keep you alive."

"Smart man," Tomás agreed. "The sea, she tests everyone eventually."

Ryder emerged from the chart room with nautical maps and historical documents spread across his arms. His green eyes found Zara immediately, and she felt that little jump in her pulse that had nothing to do with her federal mission.

"Dr. Baptiste, could you take a look at these cargo manifests?" he asked, spreading papers across the main table. "Your historical research might help us understand what we're looking for."

Zara moved to stand beside him, close enough to smell the sea salt on his skin and the faint scent of diesel and sunscreen that clung to his clothes. The papers were photocopies of Spanish colonial shipping records, faded and difficult to read, but her cover preparation had included training in historical document analysis.

"The official manifest lists general trade goods," she said, running her finger down columns of barely legible Spanish text. "Silver ingots, worked metals, agricultural products, passenger luggage."

"But?" Ryder prompted, standing close enough that she could feel the heat from his body.

"But the tonnage calculations don't match," Zara continued, studying the numbers with genuine interest. "The *Caribbean*

Star was carrying more weight than these manifests account for. Probably twenty to thirty percent more cargo than officially recorded."

"Smuggling," Jin said with matter-of-fact acceptance. "Pretty common in colonial shipping. Merchants trying to avoid Spanish taxation, passengers hiding valuables from customs officials."

"The question is what kind of valuables," Ryder said, his voice carrying undertones that suggested he had specific suspicions.

Zara looked up from the manifests to find him studying her face with those penetrating green eyes. "What makes you think it was something specific rather than general contraband?"

"Because three different treasure hunting operations have tried to find the *Caribbean Star* in the past six months," he replied. "Professional operations with serious funding and advanced equipment. That suggests the cargo was worth more than typical colonial smuggling."

Three operations. Viktor's people had been searching for the diamonds for months, which meant her federal investigation was racing against multiple criminal organizations and possibly legitimate treasure hunters who didn't know what they were really looking for.

"Any idea who the other operations were?" she asked.

"One was Russian-backed," Miguel said, his voice carrying the flat tone of someone who'd had bad experiences with Russian maritime operations. "Professional crew, military equipment, the kind of people who shoot first and ask questions later."

Viktor's people. They'd been searching for months, which meant the *Deep Explorer* sabotage had been desperation rather than the opening move in their recovery operation.

"The other two operations were harder to identify," Ryder continued. "But they were asking the same questions we are - what was the *Caribbean Star* really carrying, and where exactly did she go down?"

"And now a marine archaeology professor shows up right after a mysterious shipwreck, with research that points to the same vessel," Jin added with a slight smile. "Quite a coincidence."

Zara felt heat that had nothing to do with the Caribbean sun. These people were too smart to fool for long, and her cover story was developing holes that professional treasure hunters would notice.

"I study shipwrecks for a living," she said, trying to sound defensive rather than nervous. "The *Deep Explorer* was doing legitimate research in these waters. If that research overlapped with your treasure hunting, it's because we were both following historical evidence to the same conclusions."

"Relax, Dr. Baptiste," Ryder said with a reassuring smile. "We're not questioning your credentials. But you have to understand, in our business, coincidences can be dangerous. We've learned to be careful about new partnerships."

"Especially when those partnerships involve people who survive mysterious shipwrecks and happen to have research on the exact cargo we're hunting," Tomás added from the helm.

They suspected something, but they weren't hostile. Yet. Zara needed to give them enough truth to maintain credibility without revealing her federal identity or the full scope of what she knew about the diamonds.

"The *Caribbean Star* was carrying conflict diamonds," she said, making the decision to reveal partial information. "Stones from African mining operations, probably being smuggled to European markets through Spanish colonial trade routes."

The reaction was immediate and telling. Ryder's eyes sharpened with interest rather than surprise, Miguel nodded like he'd suspected as much, and Jin made a small sound of satisfaction.

They'd already known about the diamonds.

"How do you know that?" Ryder asked, his voice carefully neutral.

"Archaeological evidence," Zara replied, staying as close to truth as possible. "Mining records from West African Portuguese colonies, shipping manifests that don't match official cargo declarations, and contemporary accounts of unusual Spanish merchant activity in the Caribbean."

All true, and all part of the legitimate historical research that had supported her cover story. But not the whole truth about federal evidence storage and international criminal networks.

"Conflict diamonds," Miguel repeated thoughtfully. "Blood stones used to fund warfare and oppression in Africa."

"Worth millions of dollars in today's market," Jin added with technical precision. "If authenticated and properly documented."

"But illegal to sell in most international markets," Zara pointed out, testing their intentions. "Contemporary conflict diamonds are heavily regulated by international law enforcement."

"Good thing these are historical artifacts rather than contemporary contraband," Ryder said with a slight smile that didn't reach his eyes. "Proper archaeological recovery and museum documentation makes them legitimate historical specimens."

Either he was planning legitimate recovery for academic purposes, or he was very good at hiding criminal intentions.

Zara's federal training suggested the former - everything about this operation looked professional and legal, from the permits displayed in the wheelhouse to the careful documentation procedures she'd observed.

But her six months of investigating diamond trafficking had taught her that appearances could be deceiving, especially when fifty million dollars was at stake.

"Why is recovering these particular diamonds so important to you?" she asked directly.

Ryder was quiet for a long moment, green eyes studying the horizon where afternoon heat created shimmering mirages above the blue water. When he finally spoke, his voice carried personal pain that couldn't be faked.

"My brother Marcus was accused of stealing conflict diamonds from a naval evidence seizure," he said quietly. "Royal Australian Navy, special operations, the kind of man who'd die before dishonoring his service. But someone made it look like he was corrupt, and the scandal destroyed his career and his family."

"What happened to him?" Zara asked, though she suspected she already knew.

"Diving accident six months ago," Ryder replied, his voice flat with controlled grief. "Died believing the world thought he was a criminal who stole blood diamonds to fund his own lifestyle."

Six months ago. Right when the diamonds had been stolen from DEA custody in Miami. The timing was too perfect to be coincidence, which meant Marcus MacCallum had been framed by the same person who was feeding information to Viktor's organization.

"I'm sorry," Zara said, and meant it. "That's a terrible injustice."

"It was," Ryder agreed. "But if we can recover those diamonds from the *Caribbean Star* and prove they were never in Marcus's possession, we can clear his name posthumously."

"And restore his honor," Miguel added with quiet dignity.

"His children can grow up knowing their father was a hero instead of a criminal," Jin concluded.

These people weren't hunting the diamonds for profit. They were seeking justice for a dead man who'd been framed by the same corrupt federal agent that Zara was trying to expose.

Which made them natural allies, if she could figure out how to reveal her true identity without destroying the trust they were building.

"That's a worthy goal," she said carefully. "But recovering historical artifacts from international waters involves complex legal procedures. Federal agencies, maritime law enforcement, international cooperation agreements."

"We know," Ryder said with a slight smile that carried years of experience dealing with government bureaucracy. "We've done this before, Dr. Baptiste. Proper permits, legal documentation, museum partnerships, cooperation with relevant authorities."

"Even when those authorities include the same agencies that destroyed your brother's reputation?" Zara asked.

Ryder's expression hardened. "Especially then. Marcus believed in justice and proper procedure, even when the system failed him. Clearing his name means doing things the right way, no matter how difficult or frustrating the process becomes."

Honor. Integrity. Justice. Everything that federal law enforcement was supposed to represent and sometimes failed to deliver. Zara felt a stab of guilt for her own deception, mixed with growing respect for people who were willing to work within a system that had wronged them.

"The diamonds we're looking for were stolen from DEA custody six months ago," she said, making another calculated revelation. "If you recover them through legitimate archaeological procedures, you'll be returning stolen federal evidence while proving your brother's innocence."

"Assuming we can find them," Tomás said from the helm. "The *Caribbean Star* went down in deep water during hurricane conditions. The cargo could be scattered across miles of ocean floor."

"We'll find them," Ryder said with quiet confidence. "We have the research, the equipment, and the motivation. Plus, we now have a maritime archaeologist who knows what we're looking for."

The way he looked at her when he said it made Zara's pulse quicken with more than professional interest. There was attraction there, unmistakable and mutual, complicated by the deception she was maintaining and the dangerous situation they were all facing.

"How long until we reach the search coordinates?" she asked.

"Two hours," Jin replied, checking navigation displays. "We'll do preliminary survey this evening, then start diving operations tomorrow morning if conditions are favorable."

Two hours until they reached the site where fifty million dollars in conflict diamonds lay scattered across the Caribbean sea floor. Two hours until Zara had to decide whether to maintain her cover or trust these people with the truth about her federal identity.

Two hours until everything changed, one way or another.

The afternoon sun was beginning its descent toward the western horizon, painting the endless blue water in shades of gold and turquoise. The *Siren's Call* cut through gentle swells with steady purpose while her crew prepared for the most important treasure hunting operation of their careers.

And somewhere behind them, Viktor's people were probably coordinating their own approach to the *Caribbean Star* coordinates, armed with superior firepower and absolutely no regard for legal procedures or human life.

Zara stood at the bow rail, watching tropical paradise scroll past and thinking about federal obligations versus personal connections, professional duty versus human justice, and the way Ryder MacCallum's green eyes made her want things that had nothing to do with conflict diamonds or international criminal investigations.

The ocean stretched endlessly in all directions, beautiful and dangerous and full of secrets that could change everything.

Time to find out what those secrets were worth.

CHAPTER TWO

The morning sun painted the Caribbean in shades of blue and gold as the *Siren's Call* moved through gentle waves toward the *Caribbean Star* coordinates. Zara stood at the front of the boat, letting salt spray cool her dark skin while her mind worked through everything she'd learned in the past few hours.

Captain Ryder MacCallum ran a tight operation. His crew moved like they'd been working together for years, and their equipment was professional grade - not the cheap stuff she'd expect from casual treasure hunters. The charts spread across their table showed detailed ocean floor maps and historical shipping routes that would cost serious money to get.

Either these were the most thorough treasure hunters in the Caribbean, or they had backing from someone with deep pockets.

"Want the full tour?" Ryder's voice made her turn around. He stood in the doorway of the main cabin, green eyes bright in the morning light, sandy hair still damp from spray. Something about his easy confidence made her pulse speed up in ways that had nothing to do with her federal mission.

"I'd love that," she said, pushing away thoughts that had no place in an undercover operation. "I'm curious about your documentation methods."

"Jin handles our technical stuff," he said, leading her toward the back deck where the Korean woman was working with underwater metal detection equipment. "She's got the electronics and authentication gear."

Jin looked up from a complex control panel, giving Zara a friendly smile. "Dr. Baptiste, right? Ryder said you're with National Geographic."

"That's right," Zara replied, studying the expensive equipment. "This is impressive gear for private treasure hunting."

"We work with museums," Jin explained, adjusting settings with precise movements. "Authentication and documentation are crucial for legitimate archaeological work. Can't just pull artifacts from the ocean and sell them on eBay."

"The legal market pays better long-term," Miguel added, joining them from the dive equipment area. The Mexican crew member moved with the easy confidence of someone who'd spent years underwater. "Museums pay well for properly documented finds, and you don't have to worry about federal agents knocking down your door."

Zara's blood chilled a little. Random comment, or pointed reference?

"Federal oversight must be challenging," she said carefully. "DEA, Coast Guard, maritime archaeology regulations."

"It's all about proper permits and international cooperation," Ryder said, leaning against the equipment console. "We work with the system, not against it."

His tone was matter-of-fact, but Zara caught something in his expression - personal experience with federal agencies that went beyond routine permit applications.

"Have you had problems with law enforcement?" she asked.

"My brother did," Ryder said quietly. "False accusations, evidence that didn't make sense. Federal agents can destroy lives when they get fixated on the wrong people."

Zara felt a stab of guilt. How many innocent people got caught up in federal investigations? How many families got destroyed by agents like her who were so focused on their cases that they missed the bigger picture?

"I'm sorry," she said, and meant it. "That must have been hard for your family."

"It was." Ryder's jaw tightened. "Marcus died before he could clear his name. That's part of why we're out here - some discoveries can set the record straight."

The *Caribbean Star*. Whatever Ryder thought he'd find in that shipwreck was connected to his brother's case. The same diamonds she was tracking might be the key to restoring his family's honor.

This was getting complicated fast.

"Let me show you the dive setup," Miguel said, either sensing the tension or genuinely excited about the equipment.

"We've got some interesting modifications for deep-water archaeology."

The dive station was impressive - professional rebreathers, mixed-gas systems, underwater communication equipment that looked military grade. Dry suits hung in neat rows, with backup systems and emergency gear that spoke to serious attention to safety.

"You do a lot of deep diving?" Zara asked.

"Caribbean wrecks can be tricky," Miguel replied. "Strong currents, depth changes, structural problems. We've adapted some commercial diving techniques for archaeological work."

"Miguel's being modest," Jin called from the navigation station. "He was a commercial saturation diver before joining our crew. Deep-water construction, oil rig maintenance, all that heavy stuff."

"What brought you to treasure hunting?" Zara asked.

Miguel grinned. "Better stories, prettier locations, and Jin's cooking beats rig food by a mile."

"I heard that," the Korean woman called back with mock offense.

The crew dynamic felt real - professionals who'd become friends through shared adventures. Nothing like the suspicious tension she'd felt on the *Deep Explorer*. Either these people were excellent actors, or they really were what they claimed to be.

Which raised the question: why were they hunting conflict diamonds?

"Tomás handles navigation and weather forecasting," Ryder said, leading her toward the main cabin where the Brazilian crew member was studying satellite images on multiple screens.

"Dr. Baptiste," Tomás nodded politely without looking away from the displays. "Caribbean weather this time of year - she's unpredictable. Hurricane season officially ends in November, but storms can develop fast."

The screens showed real-time weather data, ocean current information, and what looked like prediction software. Professional meteorology equipment that cost more than most people made in a year.

"You're very thorough," Zara observed.

"Ocean doesn't forgive mistakes," Tomás replied in accented English. "Better to be overprepared than dead."

"Philosophy we all live by," Ryder added. "Speaking of which, what's your diving experience, Dr. Baptiste?"

Zara had to be careful here. Her federal water rescue training was extensive, but explaining advanced tactical diving skills would blow her cover story.

"I'm certified to advanced open water," she said, which was true. "Most of my underwater work has been in shallower Caribbean sites, but I'm comfortable with deeper operations."

"Good to know," Ryder said. "The *Caribbean Star* is at eighty feet, which isn't technical depth, but the currents can be tricky."

"Any idea what caused her to sink?" Zara asked.

"Hurricane Isabel last year," Jin answered from the navigation station. "Category 3 storm, caught a lot of vessels off guard. The *Caribbean Star* was trying to reach port in San Juan when the storm overwhelmed her."

"Official manifest lists general trade goods," Ryder continued, "but our research suggests she was carrying undocumented items. Passengers often brought valuable personal effects, and there's evidence of private cargo that wasn't officially recorded."

"What kind of private cargo?" Zara asked, though she suspected she knew the answer.

"Hard to say without diving the wreck," Ryder replied, but his tone suggested he had specific ideas. "Could be anything from jewelry to artwork to..." He paused. "Well, let's just say Spanish colonial trade routes were used for more than official business."

Diamonds. He was talking about diamonds without saying the word.

"That sounds fascinating," Zara said. "When do we dive?"

"Tomorrow morning, if conditions are good," Ryder said. "Today we finish the approach, check all equipment, make sure everything's ready."

The afternoon wore on with professional preparation and careful conversation. Zara helped with equipment checks and tried to learn more about her temporary partners without revealing too much about herself.

The crew was international but tight-knit. Miguel had worked construction diving in the Gulf of Mexico before joining Ryder's operation two years ago. Jin had been a commercial electronics specialist in South Korea, drawn to maritime archaeology by fascination with historical technology. Tomás had navigated commercial fishing vessels throughout the Caribbean for decades before retiring to the more relaxed pace of treasure hunting.

And Ryder himself remained an interesting puzzle. His Australian accent carried hints of naval precision, and he moved with the unconscious authority of someone used to command. The rope scars on his hands spoke of years working with marine equipment, but there was something more - a careful watchfulness that suggested experience with danger.

"You mentioned your brother earlier," Zara said as they worked together checking diving equipment. "Was he in the maritime business too?"

Ryder's hands stopped moving on the regulator he was testing. "Marcus was Royal Australian Navy. Special boat service, maritime interdiction operations."

"That sounds dangerous."

"It was," Ryder said quietly. "Drug interdiction, arms smuggling prevention, that kind of work. He was good at it, maybe too good."

"What happened?"

Ryder was silent for so long that Zara thought he wouldn't answer. When he finally spoke, his voice was carefully controlled.

"Someone accused him of stealing seized contraband. Diamonds, specifically. High-value stones that disappeared from federal custody during an operation he was involved in."

Zara's heart almost stopped. Marcus MacCallum. Royal Australian Navy. Maritime interdiction. Diamonds stolen from federal custody.

The same diamonds she'd been tracking for six months.

"The evidence was circumstantial," Ryder continued, "but convincing enough to destroy his career. He died in a diving accident six months later, before he could clear his name."

Six months ago. When the diamonds had first been stolen from DEA custody.

"I'm so sorry," Zara managed, her mind spinning. "That's a terrible tragedy."

"The worst part is knowing he was innocent," Ryder said, meeting her eyes directly. "Marcus would never have stolen anything, especially not blood diamonds tied to war crimes. But someone made it look like he did, and now his name is connected to international criminal activity."

Blood diamonds. War crimes. He knew exactly what kind of stones they were hunting.

"Is that why you're searching for the *Caribbean Star*?" Zara asked. "To clear his name?"

"If those diamonds are really on that ship," Ryder said, "and if we can prove they were stolen by someone else, it might clear Marcus's name after death."

Zara stared at him, pieces of a complex puzzle shifting into new patterns. Ryder's brother had been framed for stealing the diamonds she was tracking. The same diamonds that were now somewhere on the ocean floor, waiting to be recovered.

Which meant Ryder MacCallum was her ally, not her enemy.

But he didn't know that the federal agent sitting beside him was part of the same investigation that had destroyed his brother's reputation.

"That's a noble goal," she said carefully.

"It's family," Ryder replied simply. "Marcus died believing the world thought he was a criminal. If I can prove otherwise, his children can grow up knowing their father was a hero."

The weight of deception settled on Zara's shoulders like a lead blanket. This man was risking everything to clear his brother's name, and she was lying to him about her identity and purpose.

But she was also potentially his best chance for success. Her federal investigation had information that could prove Marcus MacCallum's innocence - if she could figure out how to reveal it without destroying the entire operation.

As evening approached, the crew settled into routine watch schedules. Miguel took the first shift at the helm, Jin monitored communications and weather updates, and Tomás prepared dinner in the boat's compact galley.

Zara found herself assigned to the second watch with Ryder - midnight to four AM, monitoring navigation and communications while the rest of the crew slept.

Which meant four hours alone with the man who was making her question everything about her mission priorities.

"You don't have to take watch duty," Ryder said as they prepared for the evening. "You're technically a passenger."

"I'm part of the crew now," Zara replied. "Besides, I've done plenty of night watches. I don't mind."

"Fair enough," he said with a slight smile. "But the midnight watch can be lonely. Just stars, ocean, and your own thoughts for company."

"Sometimes that's exactly what you need," Zara said, thinking of all the nights she'd spent awake during undercover operations, processing information and wondering if she was making the right choices.

"True enough," Ryder agreed. "I'll see you at midnight, then."

Dinner was pleasant - fresh fish that Tomás had caught during their transit, served with rice and vegetables prepared with Jin's skillful touch. The conversation flowed easily, ranging from maritime archaeology to international travel stories to good-natured arguments about the best diving locations in the Caribbean.

For a few hours, Zara almost forgot she was on a federal mission. These people felt like genuine friends, united by shared passions and mutual respect. It was the kind of crew chemistry she'd rarely experienced in law enforcement, where paranoia and competition often poisoned professional relationships.

When midnight arrived, she made her way to the main cabin where Ryder was studying weather updates on the navigation screens.

"Quiet night," he said as she settled into the co-pilot's chair. "Tomás was right about conditions - should be perfect for diving tomorrow."

"Good," Zara replied, accepting a mug of coffee from the thermal pot. "I'm excited to see the *Caribbean Star*."

"Assuming we find her," Ryder said. "Treasure hunting involves a lot of disappointment and false leads."

"But when you do find something..."

"It's like nothing else in the world," he finished with a grin. "That moment when you realize you're the first person to see something in decades or centuries - it never gets old."

They fell into comfortable conversation, sharing stories of their respective maritime experiences. Zara told carefully edited versions of her diving adventures in Miami and the Keys, while Ryder described treasure hunting expeditions throughout the Pacific and Caribbean.

The *Siren's Call* moved through gentle swells on autopilot while they talked, navigation lights creating small pools of red and green in the vast Caribbean darkness. Stars stretched overhead in patterns impossible to see from the light-polluted cities where Zara usually worked.

"What got you interested in maritime archaeology?" he asked as they watched phosphorescent waves break against the bow.

"Growing up in Miami," Zara said, which was true. "My uncle was a commercial fisherman, and he used to take me out on weekends. There's something about being on the water that just feels like home."

"I understand that," Ryder said. "My family's been connected to the ocean for generations. Commercial fishing, naval service, maritime rescue operations. The sea gets in your blood."

"Is that why you left the Royal Australian Navy?" Zara asked, taking a calculated risk.

Ryder was quiet for a moment. "You're observant."

"Military bearing is hard to hide," she replied. "Plus, you move like someone who's used to command."

"Fair enough," he said with a slight laugh. "Yes, I served. Maritime interdiction, similar to what Marcus did. Good work, important work, but..."

"But?"

"But after what happened to Marcus, I lost faith in the system," Ryder said quietly. "Federal agencies, military bureaucracy, the way good people get destroyed by politics and corruption."

Zara felt another stab of guilt. She was part of that system, part of the federal machinery that had apparently failed his brother.

"So you became a treasure hunter," she said.

"Independent contractor," he corrected with a dry smile. "I work with the system when it serves justice, and I work around it when necessary."

That was either reassuring or terrifying, depending on your perspective.

"What about you?" Ryder asked. "Ever consider leaving academia for full-time adventure?"

"Sometimes," Zara said carefully. "There's something appealing about working outside institutional constraints."

"Freedom has its advantages," he agreed. "Though it also means taking responsibility for your own decisions."

They talked through the early morning hours, sharing stories and gradually building the kind of trust that came from shared watches and honest conversation. Zara found herself relaxing in ways she hadn't during months of undercover work. Ryder was easy to talk to, intelligent without being condescending, confident without being arrogant.

And attractive in ways that had nothing to do with his sun-bleached hair and sea-green eyes. His competence was magnetic, his protectiveness appealing, his dedication to clearing his brother's name admirable.

Dangerous territory for a federal agent on assignment.

Around three AM, with the boat's autopilot maintaining their course and the ocean calm around them, the conversation turned more personal.

"Can I ask you something?" Ryder said, leaning back in his chair and studying her profile in the dim light from the instrument panel.

"Sure," Zara replied, though alarm bells were ringing in her head.

"You've been watching our wake since we left the *Deep Explorer* debris field," Ryder said quietly. "And earlier, when you thought no one was looking, you activated some kind of communication device."

Shit. Her federal training had made her cautious, but it had also made her detectable to someone with similar experience.

"I don't know what you mean," she said carefully.

"Dr. Zara Baptiste," Ryder said, turning in his chair to face her directly. "Marine archaeology professor for National Geographic. Except when Jin ran a background check, National Geographic had never heard of you."

Zara's blood went cold. "You checked?"

"Standard security protocol," Ryder said. "Your academic credentials don't exist, your publication history is fabricated, and your emergency communication device isn't standard maritime equipment."

Game over. Six months of undercover work blown by routine security checks.

"So the question is," Ryder continued, his voice still calm but with an edge of steel, "who are you really, and what do you want with the *Caribbean Star?*"

Zara weighed her options. Keep lying and hope to bluff through? Tell partial truth and try to maintain some operational security? Activate her emergency beacon and hope for federal extraction?

Or trust the man whose brother had been destroyed by the same criminal network she was hunting?

"My name really is Zara Baptiste," she said finally. "But I'm not a professor."

Ryder waited, green eyes fixed on her face in the dim instrument light.

"I'm a federal agent," she continued. "DEA. The *Caribbean Star* is carrying evidence from a major international case - fifty million dollars in conflict diamonds that were stolen from federal custody six months ago."

"Conflict diamonds," Ryder repeated, his voice carefully neutral.

"The same diamonds your brother was accused of stealing," Zara said, meeting his eyes directly. "The same diamonds that destroyed his reputation and drove him to his death."

Ryder was silent for a long moment, processing the implications.

"You're saying Marcus was framed," he said finally.

"I'm saying someone with access to federal evidence storage stole those diamonds and made your brother the fall guy," Zara replied. "My mission is to recover the diamonds and identify the real thief."

"And you think this thief is connected to whoever sabotaged the *Deep Explorer*?"

"I know he is," Zara said. "The operation I've been running for six months was blown by someone with inside access to federal communications. Someone who's been feeding information to international criminals."

Ryder stood up and moved to the helm console, checking their heading and scanning the horizon with practiced eyes.

"Any sign of pursuit?" Zara asked.

"Not yet," he replied. "But if this Viktor has the kind of resources you're describing, he'll find us eventually."

"Which is why I need to recover those diamonds and get them back to federal custody as quickly as possible," Zara said.

"Federal custody," Ryder repeated with a bitter laugh. "The same federal system that destroyed my brother's reputation."

"Not all federal agents are corrupt," Zara said quietly. "Some of us are trying to do the right thing."

Ryder turned to study her, green eyes reflecting the dim instrument lights. "And what's the right thing in this situation, Agent Baptiste?"

"Stopping Viktor Kozlov and exposing the federal mole who's been protecting him," Zara said without hesitation. "Clearing your brother's name and making sure his sacrifice wasn't wasted."

"At considerable personal risk."

"It's the job," Zara said simply.

"The job," Ryder repeated. "Not personal?"

Zara hesitated. The question carried layers of meaning that went beyond professional duty.

"It's personal now," she admitted. "Your brother was a hero who died believing the world thought he was a criminal. That's not justice."

"And what about us?" Ryder asked quietly, moving closer to where she sat at the navigation console. "This partnership we've been building - was any of that real?"

The question hit harder than she'd expected. The professional part of her mind screamed warnings about operational security and emotional compromise. But the woman sitting in the Caribbean darkness, looking up at a man who'd risked his life to rescue her, couldn't maintain that distance.

"It was real," she said softly. "More real than anything I've experienced in years of undercover work."

Ryder reached out and traced the line of her jaw with callused fingertips, his touch gentle despite the strength in his hands.

"I should be angry," he said. "You lied to me, manipulated the situation, put my crew at risk."

"You should be angry," Zara agreed, though she made no move to pull away from his touch.

"But instead, I'm impressed," Ryder continued, his thumb brushing across her lower lip. "Federal agent, maritime expert, brave enough to maintain cover under extreme pressure. And beautiful enough to make me forget about operational security."

"Ryder..."

"I know this complicates everything," he said, leaning closer until she could smell the salt air on his skin and see the flecks of gold in his green eyes. "But I need you to know - what's happening between us has nothing to do with missions or cover stories."

"What's happening between us could get us both killed," Zara whispered.

"Could," he agreed, his lips barely an inch from hers. "Or it could be the thing that keeps us alive."

The rational part of Zara's mind knew she should pull away, maintain professional distance, focus on the mission. But six months of living a lie had left her starving for something real, and the man looking at her with such intensity was offering exactly that.

She closed the distance between them.

The kiss started gentle, tentative, a question rather than a demand. Salt spray and coffee and something uniquely masculine that made her head spin. But when Zara responded, threading her fingers through his sun-bleached hair, it deepened into something more urgent.

Ryder's hands slipped to her waist, pulling her closer against his solid warmth. She could feel the steady rhythm of his heartbeat, could taste the ocean air on his lips. For a moment, the federal mission and international criminals and fifty million dollars in stolen diamonds faded away.

His mouth was warm and skilled, exploring hers with increasing confidence as she responded to his touch. The boat's gentle movement added rhythm to their connection, waves and stars and tropical night air combining to create something magical from the dangerous circumstances that had brought them together.

Zara's body responded with hunger that had nothing to do with her DEA assignment and everything to do with the competent, attractive man whose hands were mapping the curves of her body through her clothes. She could feel heat building between them, desire and attraction that had been simmering since her rescue that morning.

"God, you're beautiful," Ryder murmured against her throat, his voice rough with want. His hands moved to the hem of her t-shirt, fingers tracing the line where fabric met skin. "Your skin is incredible."

The contrast of his sun-weathered tan against her golden brown complexion was striking in the dim cabin light. Different backgrounds and experiences written in the very cells of their bodies, but somehow perfectly compatible.

"You make me feel things I shouldn't," Zara admitted breathlessly as his mouth found the sensitive spot where her neck met her shoulder. "This is supposed to be about the mission."

"Fuck the mission," Ryder said against her skin, then lifted his head to meet her eyes. "I mean that. Your mission, my mission, everything except right now."

His hands moved higher, cupping her breasts through her shirt, thumbs brushing over nipples that hardened immediately at his touch. The sensation shot straight through her body, making her arch against him with a soft sound of pleasure.

"We should stop," she whispered, even as her hands fisted in his shirt, pulling him closer.

"Should," he agreed, but his mouth was already moving lower, pressing hot kisses along her collarbone. "But I don't want to stop. Do you?"

"No," she admitted, surprised by her own honesty. "I want you to keep touching me."

"Where?" he asked, his voice low and rough with desire. "Tell me where you want my hands."

The explicit question made heat pool between her thighs, desire building with an intensity that surprised her. "Everywhere," she said honestly. "I want your hands everywhere."

Ryder's eyes darkened at her words. His hands moved to the bottom of her shirt, pulling it up and over her head with careful attention to her comfort. The Caribbean night air was warm on her bare skin, but she shivered anyway when he looked at her.

"Beautiful," he said, his voice reverent as he traced the lace edge of her bra. "Your skin looks like gold in this light."

His mouth followed the path of his hands, pressing kisses along her collarbone and down to the swell of her breasts above the lace. When his tongue traced the edge of the fabric, she gasped and arched against him.

"You taste like salt and sunshine," he murmured against her skin. "Like everything good about the ocean."

"Ryder," she breathed, her hands tangling in his hair as he found the clasp of her bra and released it with skilled fingers.

The cool night air on her bare breasts made her nipples tighten instantly, and when Ryder's mouth closed over one of them, she had to bite her lip to keep from crying out loud enough to wake the crew.

"So responsive," he murmured appreciatively, his tongue swirling around the sensitive peak. "I love the way you react to my touch."

His hands moved lower, fingers tracing the waistband of her jeans with teasing touches that made her hips move involuntarily. The space between them was charged with electricity, desire building with every caress and kiss.

"Touch me," Zara whispered, surprised by her own boldness. "Please, I need you to touch me."

Ryder's hand slipped inside her jeans, fingers finding the damp heat between her thighs through the thin fabric of her panties. The touch made her gasp and press against his hand, seeking more contact.

"You're so wet," he said against her breast, his voice filled with masculine satisfaction. "Is this for me?"

"Yes," she admitted breathlessly. "All for you."

The radio crackled with static, breaking them apart instantly.

"Mayday, mayday, this is fishing vessel *Blue Moon*, position twenty-six degrees, twelve minutes north, seventy-nine degrees, forty-five minutes west. Taking on water, engine failure, requesting immediate assistance."

Ryder was at the radio in seconds, his naval training taking over despite the obvious frustration of interrupted passion. "Fishing vessel *Blue Moon*, this is motor yacht *Siren's Call*. We copy your mayday. What is the nature of your emergency?"

Zara hurriedly pulled her shirt back on, her body still humming with unsatisfied desire but her professional instincts engaged by the emergency call.

"Hull breach from collision with debris, three souls on board, bilge pumps failing," came the desperate reply. "We're going down fast."

Ryder checked the GPS coordinates while Zara secured her bra and tried to look like they hadn't just been about to have sex on the navigation console.

"Miguel!" Ryder called toward the crew quarters. "Emergency response, now!"

The Mexican diver appeared in the cabin within seconds, fully alert despite having been asleep moments before. "What's the situation?"

"Sinking vessel, twelve miles northeast," Ryder replied, already changing course and pushing the throttles forward. "Three people in the water soon if we don't get there fast."

"Coast Guard?" Miguel asked.

"Too far out," Ryder said grimly. "We're the closest vessel."

Zara felt the boat accelerate as Ryder pushed the engines to maximum power. The professional crisis had instantly transformed him from passionate lover back to naval officer, every movement crisp and purposeful.

And she couldn't help but find that transition incredibly attractive.

"What can I do to help?" she asked.

"You said you're advanced open water certified," Ryder replied without taking his eyes off the GPS display. "How are you with emergency medical treatment?"

"Federal training includes combat medic certification," Zara said, her own professional instincts engaging. "I can handle trauma, hypothermia, near-drowning."

"Good," Ryder said, giving her a look that held promise for later. "Jin, get the medical kit and emergency blankets ready. Tomás, plot the fastest route and monitor weather conditions."

The crew moved with practiced efficiency, transforming the *Siren's Call* from treasure hunting vessel to emergency response platform. Within minutes they had spotlights rigged, rescue equipment prepared, and medical supplies staged for immediate use.

The rescue operation took forty minutes of intense, coordinated effort, but they successfully pulled three exhausted fishermen from the water and provided emergency medical care. Zara's federal training proved invaluable, treating mild hypothermia and lacerations while the crew managed the rescue logistics.

As they transferred the rescued fishermen to a Coast Guard cutter that arrived an hour later, Zara caught Ryder watching her with new appreciation.

"Nice work, Agent Baptiste," he said quietly as the last of the fishermen was helped aboard the Coast Guard vessel.

"Nice work yourself, Captain MacCallum," she replied, very aware that their interrupted encounter from earlier was still simmering between them like a promise.

"Rain check?" he asked with a slight smile that made her pulse quicken.

"Definitely," she said, matching his smile with one of her own.

As the *Siren's Call* resumed course toward the *Caribbean Star* coordinates, Zara reflected on how much had changed in a single night. Her cover was blown, her mission had become a joint operation, and she'd discovered that physical attraction could coexist with professional partnership in ways she'd never experienced.

Tomorrow they would dive for fifty million dollars in conflict diamonds. Tonight, she'd learned that some risks were worth taking, even for a federal agent who'd spent years maintaining professional distance.

The Caribbean stretched endlessly around them, dark water concealing secrets that could change everything. But for the first time in months, Zara felt like she was exactly where she needed to be.

CHAPTER THREE

Dawn painted the Caribbean in shades of pink and gold as the *Siren's Call* approached Nassau's outer harbor. The rescue operation had burned through more fuel than expected, and Ryder's professional caution demanded filling the tanks before heading to the *Caribbean Star* coordinates. Zara stood at the front of the boat, watching the Bahamian capital emerge from morning mist, her federal training automatically checking for threats and escape routes.

The city spread along the harbor like a tropical postcard - colorful buildings rising from crystal-clear water, cruise ships docked at the main terminal, fishing boats and pleasure craft creating a forest of masts and rigging. Under normal circumstances, Nassau represented safety and civilization. Today, it felt like walking into a trap.

Her encrypted communication device had received a message from Agent Martinez during the pre-dawn hours. The text was brief and coded: "Package delivery compromised. Alternate routes recommended. Maintain distance from official channels."

Translation: the federal investigation was blown, backup was compromised, and Zara was on her own in dangerous waters. The mole in the DEA had deeper access than anyone had suspected, which meant Viktor Kozlov might know her exact location and current status.

Ryder emerged from the main cabin, coffee mug in hand, green eyes scanning the harbor traffic with naval precision. His sun-weathered face showed the strain of the night's revelations and rescue operations, but his movements retained that easy competence that made her pulse quicken despite the dangerous circumstances.

The memory of their interrupted encounter at the navigation console sent heat through her body. His hands on her skin, his mouth on her breasts, the way he'd made her feel things she hadn't experienced in years of professional detachment. The radio emergency had stopped them before things went too far, but the promise of completion hung between them like electricity.

"Fuel dock is on the eastern side," he said, joining her at the rail. His voice was professional, but she caught the way his eyes lingered on her lips, remembering. "Twenty minutes to top off tanks and grab supplies, then we're out of here."

"Any sign of trouble?" Zara asked, though she'd been watching the harbor for the past hour without seeing obvious threats.

"Three fast boats anchored near the channel entrance," Ryder replied quietly. "Could be sport fishermen, could be something else. Jin's monitoring radio traffic, and Tomás is plotting emergency exit routes."

The professional paranoia of a man who'd learned not to trust easy circumstances. Zara felt a stab of guilt for bringing danger to his crew, followed by gratitude for his willingness to take those risks in pursuit of justice.

The *Siren's Call* moved through harbor traffic toward the fuel dock, passing between anchored yachts and working vessels with practiced ease. Miguel handled the dock lines while Jin monitored communications equipment for unusual chatter. The rescued fishermen had been transferred to a Coast Guard cutter hours earlier, grateful but curious about their rescuers' obvious urgency to avoid official attention.

Nassau's marina buzzed with typical Caribbean morning activity - charter boat crews preparing for tourist trips, commercial fishermen unloading night catches, yacht crews doing maintenance routines. The normalcy felt weird against the backdrop of international diamond trafficking and federal corruption that had brought Zara to these waters.

She helped Tomás secure the boat to the fuel dock while Ryder coordinated with the marina attendant. The Brazilian navigator's weather-beaten face showed concern as he scanned the surrounding vessels and shoreline structures.

"Too many people watching," he murmured in accented English, checking dock lines with unnecessary attention. "Marina workers, boat crews, tourists with cameras. Normal activity, but too much attention focused our way."

Zara followed his gaze, her federal training automatically checking the tactical environment. Most of the observers seemed genuinely casual - tourists photographing the boats, marina staff doing routine business, charter crews preparing equipment. But three men near the harbormaster's office stood out for their professional stillness and the way their eyes tracked the *Siren's Call's* movements.

White men, late thirties to early forties, wearing casual tourist clothes that didn't quite hide their military bearing. One carried a radio disguised as a cell phone, another had the telltale bulge of a concealed weapon beneath his tropical shirt, and the third maintained overwatch position with clear sightlines to multiple escape routes.

Viktor's advance team, almost certainly. The Russian arms dealer moved fast when opportunities presented themselves, and Zara's survival of the *Deep Explorer* sabotage had accelerated his timeline considerably.

"Ryder," she called softly, not taking her eyes off the three watchers. "We got company."

He glanced toward the harbormaster's office, then continued his conversation with the fuel attendant without visible reaction. Naval training included maintaining operational security under surveillance, and Captain MacCallum had clearly retained those skills despite his civilian status.

"How long for fuel?" Jin asked from the main cabin, her technical equipment monitoring multiple radio frequencies simultaneously.

"Ten minutes," the attendant replied in Caribbean-accented English. "Premium marine diesel, full tanks, yes?"

"Yes," Ryder confirmed, though Zara could see him calculating revised departure timelines in his head.

The fuel transfer proceeded with agonizing slowness while the three watchers maintained their positions near the harbor office. Additional surveillance personnel were probably positioned throughout the marina, ready to coordinate pursuit once the *Siren's Call* departed Nassau's protected waters.

Miguel finished securing dock lines and moved to help with supplies loading, his diving-trained muscles making quick work of water containers and food provisions. The Mexican crew member had grown up in coastal waters where drug trafficking and law enforcement created dangerous crosscurrents, and his street-smart awareness complemented the crew's maritime expertise.

"Fast boats at channel entrance are moving," Jin reported from the main cabin, her electronics monitoring maritime traffic control frequencies. "Three vessels, heading toward inner harbor in formation."

"Coordinated approach," Zara observed, watching the distant boats change from casual anchorage to tactical positioning. Her Little Haiti upbringing had taught her to recognize when predators were moving into hunting formation. "They trying to box us in before we reach open water."

"Standard interdiction pattern," Ryder agreed, his voice carrying the flat calm of naval combat experience. "Block the main channel, force target vessel into secondary waterways where pursuit boats have maneuverability advantages."

The fuel transfer completed with mechanical precision, but Zara could feel time pressure building like storm clouds on the horizon. Viktor's people were professional enough to coordinate their assault, which meant the *Siren's Call* needed to be moving before those fast boats reached optimal attack positions.

"Cast off," Ryder ordered as the fuel attendant disconnected the diesel lines. "All ahead full once we clear the dock."

Miguel and Tomás handled dock lines with practiced efficiency while Jin powered up navigation and communication systems. The *Siren's Call's* engines rumbled to life, twin diesels providing the reliable power that might make the difference between escape and capture in the next few minutes.

Zara positioned herself where she could observe the harbor approaches while staying clear of the crew's maneuvering activities. Her federal training included maritime tactics and pursuit evasion, but these waters belonged to Ryder's expertise. The best thing she could do was provide intelligence and stay ready to assist with whatever crisis developed.

The three watchers near the harbor office had moved closer to the waterfront, maintaining visual contact with the departing treasure hunting vessel. One spoke into his disguised radio while the others began walking purposefully toward a sleek speedboat moored at the adjacent pier.

"Pursuit team launching," Zara called to the main cabin as the *Siren's Call* cleared the fuel dock and began accelerating toward the channel entrance.

"Copy that," Ryder replied, pushing the throttles forward and sending the boat surging through harbor traffic. "Jin, monitor all emergency frequencies. Miguel, prepare dive equipment for emergency deployment. Tomás, plot evasion courses through the shallow reefs."

The crew responded with military precision, transforming from casual treasure hunters to professional tactical unit within seconds. Whatever their individual backgrounds, these people had worked together long enough to function as an integrated team under pressure.

The harbor channel stretched ahead like a nautical highway, marked by navigational buoys and bordered by coral reefs that could shred an unwary vessel's hull. The three fast boats from the channel entrance were converging on an intercept course, their powerful engines creating rooster tails of spray as they accelerated toward contact.

Zara estimated their speed at forty knots, compared to the *Siren's Call's* maximum of maybe thirty-five. Math and physics favored the pursuers, but local knowledge and tactical experience might balance those advantages.

"Shallow water ahead," Tomás announced from the navigation station, studying detailed charts that showed reef formations and depth soundings throughout the area. "Local fishing grounds, many coral heads, narrow passages between shoals."

"Perfect," Ryder replied with grim satisfaction, adjusting course toward water that would challenge any captain unfamiliar with Bahamian reef systems.

The lead pursuit boat was less than half a mile away now, close enough to identify individual crew members and weapons mounted on the bow. Zara counted at least four men aboard, all wearing tactical gear and carrying automatic weapons. Professional military contractors, not local criminals hired for quick intimidation.

Viktor Kozlov took his diamond recovery seriously.

"They're signaling us to stop," Jin reported, monitoring radio communications. "Official-sounding demands, but no valid authority identification."

"Ignore them," Ryder ordered, pushing deeper into the reef system where chart knowledge would determine survival. "Miguel, stand by with emergency equipment."

The first gunshots shattered the morning calm like thunder, automatic weapons fire splitting the air with deadly precision. Hot brass casings glinted in tropical sunlight as bullets chewed foam from waves barely ten feet from their stern. Zara hit the deck hard, her Little Haiti street instincts kicking in before her federal training even registered the threat. The sharp crack of high-velocity rounds mixed with the smell of gunpowder carried on salt air.

"Warning shots!" she called to Ryder, who was navigating between coral heads with absolute concentration.

"Won't stay warnings long!" he replied, threading the boat through a passage barely wider than their beam. "They want us alive for questioning, but they'll start targeting engines soon!"

More gunfire erupted from the pursuing speedboats, this time aimed at the water near their stern. The message was clear - stop now, or face escalating violence that would end with capture or death.

The *Siren's Call* emerged from the narrow coral passage into a shallow lagoon surrounded by mangrove islands and sand bars. Ryder's hands gripped the wheel with white-knuckled intensity as twin diesel engines screamed at maximum power, their wake churning the pristine water into foam. The sweet scent of tropical flowers mixed with diesel exhaust and gun smoke, creating a surreal contrast between paradise and warfare.

"Two boats following us through the passage," Miguel reported from the stern, watching their wake for signs of pursuit. "Third boat heading around the reef system, probably trying to cut us off at the far end."

"Classic pincer movement," Zara observed, her tactical training analyzing the developing situation. Her federal experience with drug interdiction operations had included similar scenarios. "They trying to box us in where superior firepower can overwhelm evasive maneuvering."

"Then we don't let them complete the pincer," Ryder decided, studying the navigation chart with quick glances while maintaining visual contact with reef markers ahead.

He swung the boat hard to port, heading toward what looked like solid mangrove coastline but which the chart revealed as a narrow creek entrance hidden among the vegetation. The *Siren's Call* disappeared into the mangrove tunnel like a fish diving into coral, leaving barely a ripple to mark their passage.

The mangrove creek was a green cathedral of twisted roots and hanging branches, barely wide enough for their beam and shallow enough that the wrong turn could ground them permanently. Ryder navigated by instinct and chart memory, following a waterway that few people knew existed.

Behind them, the sound of pursuit boats grew fainter as Viktor's people searched the open lagoon for their vanished target. The mangrove canopy provided perfect concealment, but it also limited their options to a single narrow channel with unknown exit points.

"Where this creek lead?" Zara asked quietly, not wanting her voice to carry through the still air. Her Miami accent was thicker with stress.

"Small cove on the back side of the island," Tomás replied in a whisper, consulting charts that showed the mangrove system in detail. "Hidden beach, deep water anchorage, multiple escape routes if we need them."

"If the pursuit boats don't find the entrance," Jin added, monitoring radio traffic through headphones to avoid broadcasting their position.

The creek wound through increasingly dense vegetation, with overhanging branches occasionally scraping the boat's superstructure and roots extending into water dark as coffee. Tropical birds called from hidden perches while iguanas watched their passage with ancient indifference. Paradise and danger intertwined in the way that defined Caribbean waters.

After twenty minutes of careful navigation, the mangrove tunnel opened into a perfect hidden cove - white sand beach backed by palm trees, crystal-clear water deep enough for safe anchoring, and coral formations that would challenge any unwary pursuit vessel. The kind of secret refuge that treasure hunters and smugglers had used for centuries.

"Engines off," Ryder ordered as they entered the cove. "We'll anchor and wait for the pursuit to move on."

The sudden silence felt profound after hours of engine noise and tactical tension. Natural sounds returned - wave action against coral, palm fronds rustling in the trade wind, tropical birds resuming their morning routines. The *Siren's Call* swung slowly on her anchor rode while her crew processed the morning's events.

"Think they'll find us here?" Miguel asked, scanning the mangrove entrance they'd used to reach this sanctuary.

"Eventually," Ryder replied with professional realism. "But it'll take time, and time gives us options."

Zara moved to the stern rail, studying the hidden cove while her federal training evaluated their tactical situation. Excellent defensive position with multiple escape routes, but limited long-term sustainability. They had supplies for several days, but Viktor's resources could maintain pressure indefinitely.

The adrenaline from their escape was still coursing through her system, making her hyperaware of everything - the way sunlight filtered through palm fronds, the sound of water lapping against white sand, the heat building in her body that had nothing to do with the Caribbean climate.

"We can't stay here forever," she said, voicing what everyone was thinking. "Sooner or later, we have to reach the *Caribbean Star* coordinates."

"Agreed," Ryder said, joining her at the rail. His presence made her pulse quicken, memories of their interrupted encounter mixing with the adrenaline rush of survival. "But we also can't lead Viktor's people directly to the diamond site. That would eliminate any advantage we might have."

"So what's the plan?" Jin asked from the main cabin, where she continued monitoring communication frequencies for signs of pursuit coordination.

Ryder was quiet for a moment, green eyes studying the cove's crystal-clear water with the kind of focused attention that preceded tactical decisions. When he finally spoke, his voice carried naval authority mixed with treasure hunter pragmatism.

"We wait until dark," he decided. "Let Viktor's people exhaust themselves searching the reef system. Then we slip out through the back channels and approach the *Caribbean Star* site from an unexpected direction."

"Night navigation through coral reefs," Tomás observed with the concern of a professional navigator. "Dangerous even with GPS and chart plotters."

"Less dangerous than daylight assault by international criminals," Zara pointed out, though she shared the Brazilian's concern about night reef navigation.

The afternoon heat became oppressive in the sheltered cove, but first, the adrenaline from their escape needed an outlet. Zara found herself standing at the stern rail, hands still shaking slightly from the morning's violence. The crystal-clear water lapped peacefully against white sand, a perfect contrast to the chaos they'd just survived.

"You okay?" Ryder's voice was soft as he joined her, close enough that she could smell the salt spray on his skin mixed with something uniquely masculine - sun and sea and strength.

"Just processing," she said, though her pulse was still elevated for reasons that had nothing to do with their narrow escape. "Been a minute since people shot at me with that kind of commitment."

"Welcome to treasure hunting," he said with a slight smile, but his green eyes were serious as they studied her face. "Most archaeology expeditions don't include high-speed chases."

"Most DEA operations don't include kissing fine Australian sea captains either," Zara replied, then immediately felt heat rise in her cheeks. The words had slipped out before her professional control could stop them.

Ryder's smile became genuine, transforming his weathered features. "So you were thinking about the kiss."

"Hard not to think about it when we almost died before…" She trailed off, suddenly aware of how close he was standing, how the tropical heat made his t-shirt cling to his chest, how his eyes held flecks of gold that matched the afternoon sunlight.

"Before what?" he asked quietly, stepping closer until she could feel the warmth radiating from his body.

"Before I could find out what comes next," she admitted.

The space between them disappeared as he cupped her face with hands that were gentle despite their rope scars and calluses. This kiss was different from the interrupted moment during night watch - deeper, more urgent, fed by shared danger and the intoxicating realization that they were alive and safe and alone.

Zara's federal training screamed warnings about operational security, but her body responded to six months of living a lie by embracing something beautifully, dangerously real. She pressed closer, her hands fisting in his shirt as he backed her against the rail.

"We should go to the beach," Ryder murmured against her lips, his voice rough with want.

"We should," she agreed breathlessly, though neither of them moved to break the contact.

The white sand beach beckoned like paradise, isolated and perfect, surrounded by mangrove walls that provided complete privacy. Ryder's hands slipped to her waist, lifting her easily from the boat to the shallow water, then carrying her through the crystal-clear lagoon to the shore.

The sand was powder-soft beneath her feet as he set her down, warm from the tropical sun but cooled by trade wind rustling through palm fronds overhead. This was the Caribbean of postcards and dreams - turquoise water, white beach, swaying palms - but the man looking at her with such intensity made it feel like something much more personal.

"You sure about this?" Ryder asked, though his hands were already tracing the line of her arms, sending electricity through her nerves.

"Nothing's been sure since my ship went down yesterday," Zara replied, her Miami accent heavy with emotion. "But this feels right."

He kissed her again, slower this time, exploring rather than claiming. Her protective braids had loosened during the morning's chaos, and he carefully removed the elastic ties, letting her natural hair fall around her shoulders like a dark cloud. The gesture was intimate and careful, acknowledging the cultural significance of Black women's hair in a way that touched her more deeply than mere passion.

"Beautiful," he murmured, threading his fingers through the textured strands with reverent attention.

The afternoon sun painted golden highlights on her brown skin as they sank onto the warm sand together, mouths hungry and hands exploring with increasing urgency. Six months of deception fell away as Zara let herself be completely honest for the first time since beginning this assignment.

Ryder's touch was confident but patient, mapping the curves of her body through clothing that suddenly felt like barriers to the connection they both craved. When she tugged impatiently at his shirt, he helped her remove it, revealing the sun-bronzed chest and rope-scarred hands of a man who'd spent his life working with the ocean.

The contrast of their skin tones in the tropical light was breathtaking - her golden brown against his weathered tan, different backgrounds and experiences written in the very cells of their bodies but somehow perfectly complementary.

"Damn, you're gorgeous," he breathed as she pressed kisses along his collarbone, tasting salt and sunshine and something essentially masculine.

"Keep talking like that and I might start believing you," she teased, but her voice caught as his hands found the hem of her shirt and began lifting it with careful attention to her comfort level.

The afternoon heat made clothing feel oppressive anyway, and when cool ocean breeze touched her bare skin, Zara sighed with pure pleasure. Ryder's eyes darkened as he took in the sight of her - all golden brown curves and confident feminine strength - before leaning down to press kisses along her throat.

"I can't believe yesterday you were drowning in a storm, and today..." he said against her skin.

"Today we're alive," she finished, arching into his touch as his mouth found the sensitive spot where her neck met her shoulder. "Today we're safe. Today we're here."

His hands moved to cup her breasts through her lace bra, thumbs brushing over nipples that hardened immediately at his touch. The sensation shot straight through her body, making her arch against him with a soft moan of pleasure.

"You like that?" he asked, his voice low and rough with desire.

"Yes," she whispered, surprised by her own boldness. "I like your hands on me."

"Where else do you want my hands?" he asked, echoing their interrupted conversation from the night before.

"Everywhere," she said honestly, heat pooling between her thighs. "I want you to touch me everywhere."

Ryder's eyes darkened at her words. His hands moved to unclasp her bra, freeing her breasts to the warm afternoon air. When his mouth closed over one nipple, she had to bite her lip to keep from crying out.

"So responsive," he murmured appreciatively, his tongue swirling around the sensitive peak. "I love watching you react to my mouth."

His hands moved lower, fingers working at the button of her jeans with practiced skill. When he slipped his hand inside, finding the damp heat between her thighs through her panties, she gasped and pressed against his touch.

"Shit, you're wet," he said with masculine satisfaction, his fingers stroking her through the thin fabric. "Is this all for me?"

"All for you," she confirmed breathlessly, her hips moving involuntarily against his hand.

He worked her jeans and panties down her legs, leaving her completely naked on the white sand. The tropical sun on her bare skin felt incredible, but not as incredible as the way Ryder looked at her like she was the most beautiful thing he'd ever seen.

"Perfect," he said, his hands mapping every curve and hollow. "Your skin looks like gold in this light."

When his mouth followed the path of his hands, pressing kisses down her stomach toward the junction of her thighs, Zara thought she might lose her mind from the anticipation.

"Tell me what you want," he said, his breath warm against her most sensitive skin.

"Your mouth," she said without shame, her federal training in direct communication serving her well in this very different context. "I want your mouth on me."

"Here?" he asked, pressing a soft kiss to her inner thigh.

"Higher," she demanded, her voice rough with need.

When his tongue finally found her clit, she cried out and fisted her hands in the sand, her back arching off the ground. He was skilled and thorough, alternating between gentle licks and firm pressure that had her writhing beneath him.

"Taste so good," he murmured against her flesh. "Like sunshine and ocean salt."

His fingers joined his mouth, sliding inside her slick heat while his tongue continued its assault on her clit. The dual sensations had her climbing toward climax with embarrassing speed.

"Ryder," she gasped, her thighs trembling. "I'm gonna..."

"Come for me," he encouraged, his fingers curving to hit that perfect spot inside her. "Let me hear you."

The orgasm hit her like a tidal wave, pleasure crashing through her body as she cried out his name. He didn't stop, prolonging her climax until she was shaking and oversensitive.

When he finally lifted his head, his lips were glistening with her juices, and his eyes were dark with satisfied desire.

"That was beautiful," he said, crawling up her body to capture her mouth in a kiss that let her taste herself on his lips.

"Your turn," she said, her hands working at his belt with urgent fingers.

She pushed his jeans down his hips, freeing his hard cock to the afternoon air. He was impressive - thick and long and already leaking pre-cum from the tip.

"I want to taste you too," she said, wrapping her hand around his shaft.

"Next time," he said, his voice strained. "Right now I need to be inside you."

He positioned himself between her thighs, the head of his cock nudging at her entrance. The contrast of his pale skin against her dark thighs was striking, and she found herself captivated by the visual.

"You ready for me?" he asked, his voice tight with restraint.

"So ready," she confirmed, wrapping her legs around his waist.

He pushed inside slowly, stretching her walls around his thickness. The sensation was incredible - fullness and pressure and the intimate connection of their bodies joining completely.

"Fuck, you feel amazing," he groaned, bottoming out inside her. "So tight and wet."

"Move," she demanded, her nails digging into his shoulders. "I need you to move."

He set a steady rhythm, thrusting deep and hitting all the right spots. The sand beneath them was soft and warm, the ocean breeze cooling their heated skin, and the sound of waves provided a natural soundtrack to their lovemaking.

"Harder," she gasped, her body already building toward another climax. "I can take it."

He obliged, picking up the pace and driving into her with more force. The new angle had him hitting her G-spot with every thrust, and she could feel herself spiraling toward release again.

"Touch yourself," he commanded, his voice rough. "I want to watch you come while I'm inside you."

She slipped her hand between their bodies, fingers finding her clit and rubbing in tight circles. The added stimulation was exactly what she needed, and within moments she was coming again, her inner walls clenching around his cock.

"That's it," he encouraged, his thrusts becoming erratic as her climax triggered his own. "Squeeze my cock just like that."

He buried himself deep inside her as he came, his release pulsing hot and thick into her body. They collapsed together on the sand, breathing hard and covered in a sheen of sweat despite the ocean breeze.

"That was incredible," Zara said after she'd caught her breath.

"Better than incredible," Ryder agreed, pressing a soft kiss to her temple. "That was perfect."

They lay entwined on the warm sand for a while, skin cooling in the trade wind while their heartbeats gradually returned to normal. The hidden cove stretched around them like paradise, crystal-clear water and white sand and tropical vegetation creating the perfect setting for their passionate encounter.

Eventually they cleaned up in the shallow water and returned to the boat, sand-dusted and sun-kissed and carrying the satisfied glow of people who'd taken something beautiful from a day that had started with violence. The crew made no comment about their afternoon absence, but Jin's knowing smile and Miguel's satisfied nod suggested their absence hadn't gone unnoticed.

"Radio chatter's picking up," Jin reported from the communications station as evening approached. "Viktor's people are expanding their search pattern. Getting frustrated at losing us."

"How long before they try different tactics?" Ryder asked, settling into tactical planning mode despite their recent intimacy.

"Hard to say," Jin replied. "But they're talking about bringing in additional resources. Helicopter support, maybe more boats."

"Then we stick to the plan," Ryder decided. "Wait for darkness, then make our run to the *Caribbean Star* coordinates."

The sun was setting over the Caribbean, painting the hidden cove in shades of orange and gold. Soon they would be running dark through dangerous waters, relying on stealth and local knowledge to avoid detection while pursuing fifty million dollars in conflict diamonds.

But for now, Zara was content to sit beside Ryder at the helm, their bodies still humming with satisfaction from their passionate encounter on the beach. Whatever dangers lay ahead, they would face them together as partners in every sense of the word.

The ocean stretched endlessly beyond their hidden refuge, dark water concealing secrets that could change everything. Time to find out what those secrets were worth.

CHAPTER FOUR

The Caribbean night was black as ink when the *Siren's Call* slipped out of her hidden cove like a ghost. No navigation lights, engines at quarter throttle, every piece of equipment secured to avoid noise. Zara stood beside Ryder at the helm, watching him navigate by starlight and memory through reef channels that could rip their hull open with one wrong move.

Her body still hummed with satisfaction from their afternoon on the beach. The taste of him lingered in her mouth, the feel of his hands on her skin burned into memory. But now, heading toward fifty million dollars in blood diamonds, reality was setting in hard.

She was falling for a man she'd been lying to. And when he found out the whole truth about her federal mission, it might destroy everything between them.

"Nervous, love?" Ryder asked softly, his Australian accent thicker in the darkness. "You're wound tight as a spring."

"Just thinking," Zara replied, her Miami accent slipping through despite her best efforts to stay professional. "About what we might find down there tomorrow."

"Fair dinkum, it's gonna change everything," he said, adjusting their heading around a coral head that appeared like a sleeping whale in their path. "Either we clear Marcus's name, or we learn something that makes this whole bloody mess even worse."

The pain in his voice when he mentioned his dead brother made Zara's chest tight. Marcus MacCallum had been destroyed by the same corrupt federal agent she was hunting.

If she could help clear his name while exposing the mole, maybe some good would come from all this deception.

"Tell me about him," she said quietly. "Marcus. What was he like?"

Ryder was silent for so long she thought he wouldn't answer. When he finally spoke, his voice was rough with emotion.

"Best man I ever knew," he said simply. "Three years older, Royal Australian Navy since he was eighteen. Special operations, maritime interdiction, the kind of bloke who'd die before letting his mates down."

"Sounds like you looked up to him."

"Course I did. He was everything I wanted to be - honorable, brave, dedicated to doing right by people who couldn't protect themselves." Ryder's hands tightened on the wheel. "When those diamonds went missing from federal custody, and the evidence pointed to Marcus... it broke something in our family that can't be fixed."

Zara felt like someone was squeezing her heart with both hands. The "federal custody" those diamonds had been stolen from was her own agency. Her own people had destroyed this man's brother and family.

"How did he die?" she asked, though she was afraid of the answer.

"Diving accident," Ryder said flatly. "Solo dive on a wreck off Queensland, equipment failure, never came back up. But I know Marcus like I know my own heartbeat. He was too good a diver for simple equipment failure."

"You think someone killed him?"

"I think he was getting close to proving his innocence," Ryder said with quiet certainty. "And someone made sure he never got the chance."

The weight of her deception felt like it might crush her. This man trusted her, had made love to her on a Caribbean beach, was risking his life to help her mission. And she was keeping secrets that could tear apart everything between them.

But she was also potentially his best chance for justice. Her federal investigation could prove Marcus MacCallum's innocence - if she could figure out how to reveal it without destroying the trust they'd built.

"Contact on radar," Jin reported quietly from the navigation station, her Korean accent adding precision to the whispered words. "Small vessel, two miles southeast, moving parallel to our course."

"Viktor's people?" Zara asked, her federal training instantly alert.

"Could be," Ryder replied, studying the radar display with naval focus. "Or could be local fishermen running night lines. Hard to tell without visual confirmation."

"I'm monitoring radio frequencies," Jin continued, adjusting her headset. "No chatter yet, but they're maintaining electronic silence if it's hostile."

The night hours crawled by with tense vigilance as the *Siren's Call* worked her way through reef systems and shipping channels toward the *Caribbean Star* coordinates. Every radar contact brought adrenaline, every unusual sound made the crew check their weapons and emergency equipment.

Miguel and Tomás took turns on watch while Jin monitored communications and weather data. The Brazilian navigator's decades of experience reading Caribbean conditions proved invaluable as they navigated around a weather system developing to the north.

"Storm building," Tomás reported, studying satellite imagery on multiple screens. "Not hurricane strength, but strong enough to make diving dangerous if it moves south."

"How long do we have?" Ryder asked.

"Twelve hours, maybe fourteen if the system moves slower than predicted," Tomás replied. "After that, surface conditions will be too rough for safe diving operations."

Twelve hours to find, dive, and recover fifty million dollars in conflict diamonds before weather forced them to abandon the site. And that assumed Viktor's people didn't find them first.

"ETA to coordinates?" Zara asked.

"Two hours at current speed," Ryder confirmed. "We'll be on site before dawn, which gives us maximum daylight for diving operations."

Around four AM, as false dawn began lightening the eastern horizon, Zara found herself alone with Ryder at the helm while the rest of the crew caught a few hours of sleep before the diving operation began.

The intimacy of shared watch duty, the gentle movement of the boat beneath them, and the memory of their passionate encounter on the beach created a cocoon of connection that made her want to tell him everything.

"Ryder," she began, then stopped. How do you tell someone you've been lying about your identity since the moment you met them?

"Something on your mind, love?" he asked, his green eyes studying her face in the dim light from the instrument panel.

"Earlier, when I told you I was DEA," she said carefully, "I didn't tell you the whole story."

"Figured as much," he replied with a slight smile. "Federal agents don't usually reveal everything in the first conversation."

"This is different." Zara took a deep breath, knowing this could change everything between them. "The agent who stole those diamonds - the one who framed your brother - I think I know who it is."

Ryder's hands stilled on the wheel. "You know who destroyed Marcus?"

"My handler, Agent Sarah Martinez," Zara said, the words tasting bitter in her mouth. "She's been feeding information to Viktor's organization, compromising operations, covering tracks. The evidence has been building for months."

"Your own handler," Ryder said quietly. "The person you're supposed to trust most in the whole bloody system."

"Yeah." Zara's voice was thick with emotion. "She's been playing both sides, taking money from arms dealers while pretending to investigate them. And when your brother got too close to the truth..."

"She made him disappear," Ryder finished, his voice flat with controlled rage.

"I can't prove it yet," Zara continued. "But all the pieces fit. Martinez had access to the evidence storage where the diamonds were kept. She knew Marcus was investigating the theft. She could have arranged the diving 'accident' that killed him."

Ryder was quiet for a long time, staring out at the dark ocean while processing the implications.

"So this mission of yours," he finally said. "It's not just about recovering stolen diamonds."

"It's about exposing the corruption that destroyed your brother," Zara confirmed. "And making sure the people responsible pay for what they did."

"Including your own colleague."

"Especially my own colleague," Zara said fiercely. "Martinez took an oath to protect people and serve justice. Instead, she sold out to war criminals and let good men die for her greed."

The raw emotion in her voice seemed to convince Ryder more than any logical argument could have. He reached over and took her hand, his calloused fingers intertwining with hers.

"You could have kept this to yourself," he said quietly. "Used me and my crew to recover the diamonds, then disappeared back to your federal life."

"I thought about it," Zara admitted honestly. "For about five seconds. Then I realized I'd rather have you as a partner than as someone I betrayed."

"Partner," he repeated, testing the word. "In the professional sense?"

"In every sense," she replied, meeting his eyes directly. "Professional, personal, whatever this is between us."

"What is this between us?" Ryder asked, his voice carrying undertones that made her pulse quicken despite the serious conversation.

"Complicated," Zara said with a slight smile. "Dangerous. Probably tactically inadvisable."

"But?"

"But real," she finished. "More real than anything I've felt in years."

The space between them seemed to shrink as he leaned closer, his free hand coming up to cup her face with gentle pressure.

"I should be furious with you," he said, his thumb brushing across her cheek. "More lies, more secrets, more federal complications."

"You should be," she agreed, though she made no move to pull away from his touch.

"Instead, I'm thinking about how brave you are," he continued, his Australian accent making the words sound like poetry. "Taking on corrupt agents, international criminals, risking everything for justice."

"I'm thinking about this afternoon," she said honestly. "About how good you made me feel. About how much I want you to make me feel that way again."

The hunger that flashed in his green eyes made heat pool between her thighs, desire building despite the tactical situation and serious conversation.

"The crew's asleep," he said, his voice rough with want.

"The boat's on autopilot," she replied, already moving closer.

"We should be focused on the mission," he said, even as his hands found the hem of her t-shirt.

"We should," she agreed breathlessly, helping him pull the shirt over her head.

The main cabin was dimly lit by instrument panels, creating pools of red and green light that painted their skin in jewel tones. The gentle movement of the boat added rhythm to their movements as they came together with the desperate hunger of people who might not survive the next twenty-four hours.

Ryder's hands were everywhere at once - tracing the curve of her waist, cupping her breasts through her bra, sliding down to grip her ass and pull her against his hardening cock. The feel of his desire pressing against her through their clothes made her gasp and arch into his touch.

"You're so fucking beautiful," he murmured against her throat, his Australian accent thick with arousal. "Been thinking about touching you again since we left the beach."

"Then touch me," she challenged, her Miami accent sliding into the words. "Touch me everywhere, *papi*."

The Spanish endearment made him growl low in his throat as he spun her around and pressed her against the navigation console, his body hard and warm against her back.

"Here?" he asked, his hands sliding up her stomach to cup her breasts. "With my crew sleeping just down the hallway?"

"Everywhere," she confirmed, pressing her ass back against his erection. "I don't care who might hear."

His teeth found the sensitive spot where her neck met her shoulder, biting gently while his hands made quick work of her bra clasp. When the lace fell away and cool night air hit her nipples, she had to bite her lip to keep from moaning loud enough to wake the crew.

"So responsive," he murmured appreciatively, his fingers rolling her nipples to hard peaks. "I love how your body reacts to me."

"Keep talking like that and I'm gonna come before you even get my pants off," she warned, pressing back against him harder.

"Is that a challenge?" he asked, one hand sliding down to work at her jeans button.

"It's a promise," she replied, then gasped as his hand slipped inside her pants to find her already wet and ready.

"Fuck, you're soaked," he said with masculine satisfaction, his fingers stroking through her slick folds. "All this for me?"

"All for you," she confirmed breathlessly. "Always for you."

He worked her jeans and panties down her legs, leaving her naked from the waist down while he remained fully clothed behind her. The contrast was erotic and empowering - she felt exposed and vulnerable but also completely desired.

"Spread your legs," he commanded softly, his hands guiding her thighs apart. "I want to see how wet you are for me."

She complied, bracing her hands on the navigation console while he explored her with gentle fingers. The position left her completely open to his touch, her most intimate places accessible to his skilled hands.

"Beautiful," he murmured, his fingers tracing her folds with reverent attention. "You're glistening in this light."

When he slipped two fingers inside her, she couldn't hold back a soft cry of pleasure. He found her G-spot immediately, stroking with practiced skill while his thumb circled her clit.

"That's it," he encouraged, his voice rough with arousal. "Let me hear how good it feels."

"So good," she gasped, her hips moving involuntarily against his hand. "Don't stop, please don't stop."

He increased the pressure and rhythm, his fingers working inside her while his thumb maintained steady pressure on her clit. The dual stimulation had her climbing toward climax embarrassingly fast.

"You're close," he observed, his free hand sliding up to play with her nipples. "I can feel you getting tighter around my fingers."

"Yeah," she panted, her whole body trembling with approaching release. "I'm gonna come."

"Do it," he commanded. "Come all over my hand."

The orgasm hit her like lightning, pleasure crashing through her body as she cried out his name. Her inner walls clenched around his fingers while waves of sensation made her legs shake and her vision blur.

He didn't stop, prolonging her climax until she was gasping and oversensitive, pushing weakly at his hand.

"Too much," she protested, though her body was already responding to his continued touch.

"Never too much," he disagreed, his fingers still moving inside her. "I want to feel you come again."

"I can't," she said, even as heat began building again between her thighs.

"You can," he said confidently. "You're gonna come for me again, and then I'm gonna fuck you right here against this console."

The crude words sent fresh arousal through her system, and she felt herself getting wetter around his fingers.

"You like that idea," he observed with satisfaction. "You like the thought of me bending you over and taking you hard."

"Yes," she admitted shamelessly. "I want your cock inside me."

"Soon," he promised, his fingers finding that perfect spot again. "But first, I want to feel you fall apart again."

It took longer this time, but his skilled touch and dirty words eventually pushed her over the edge into another powerful climax. This one left her shaking and breathless, completely dependent on his strength to keep her upright.

"That's my girl," he murmured approvingly, finally withdrawing his fingers. "Now it's my turn."

She heard the sound of his belt buckle and zipper, then felt the hot length of his cock pressing against her from behind. He was thick and hard, already leaking pre-cum that made her even slicker.

"You ready for me?" he asked, the head of his cock nudging at her entrance.

"So ready," she confirmed, bracing herself against the console. "I need you inside me."

He pushed inside slowly, stretching her walls around his impressive girth. The sensation was incredible - fullness and pressure and the intimate connection of their bodies joining completely.

"Christ, you feel amazing," he groaned, bottoming out inside her. "So tight and wet and perfect."

"Move," she demanded, pushing back against him. "I need you to fuck me."

He obliged, setting a steady rhythm that had him hitting all the right spots. The navigation console creaked slightly with their movements, but neither of them cared about anything except the pleasure building between them.

"Harder," she gasped, her body already climbing toward another peak. "I can take it."

He increased the pace and force, driving into her with the kind of controlled power that spoke to his naval training and natural dominance. Each thrust sent pleasure shooting through her system, building toward what felt like it might be the most intense orgasm of her life.

"Touch yourself," he commanded, his voice strained with effort. "I want to feel you come on my cock."

She slipped her hand between her legs, fingers finding her clit and rubbing in tight circles. The added stimulation was exactly what she needed, and within moments she was coming again, her inner walls clenching around his shaft.

"Fuck, yes," he groaned, his rhythm becoming erratic as her climax triggered his own. "That's it, squeeze me just like that."

He buried himself deep inside her as he came, his release pulsing hot and thick into her body. They stayed connected for long moments afterward, breathing hard and covered in a sheen of sweat despite the cool night air.

"That was incredible," Zara said after she'd caught her breath.

"Better than incredible," Ryder agreed, pressing a soft kiss to her shoulder. "That was perfect."

They cleaned up quickly and got dressed, professional awareness returning as they resumed their watch duties. But the connection between them felt deeper now, strengthened by physical intimacy and emotional honesty.

"Coordinates coming up," Tomás called from the navigation station as the crew began stirring for the morning's diving operations.

"Right then," Ryder said, his voice carrying naval authority mixed with treasure hunter enthusiasm. "Time to see what secrets the *Caribbean Star* has been keeping."

The sun was rising over the Caribbean, painting the endless blue water in shades of gold and turquoise. Somewhere beneath them, fifty million dollars in conflict diamonds waited to be recovered, along with evidence that could clear a dead man's name and expose international corruption.

But first, they had to find the wreck, dive to it safely, and recover the cargo before Viktor's people or bad weather ended their mission permanently.

Zara stood beside Ryder at the helm as the *Siren's Call* approached the search coordinates, her body still humming with satisfaction from their encounter but her mind focused on the dangerous work ahead.

Whatever secrets lay beneath the Caribbean waters, they were about to uncover them together.

The ocean stretched endlessly in all directions, keeping its secrets until someone was brave enough to dive deep and bring them to light.

Today was that day.

The *Caribbean Star* coordinates looked like every other patch of Caribbean water - endless blue stretching to the horizon, gentle swells rolling beneath tropical sun, no indication that a Spanish merchant vessel lay broken on the bottom eighty feet below.

Miguel was already suiting up for the initial reconnaissance dive, checking his rebreather system and underwater metal detector with the methodical precision of someone who'd learned that sloppy preparation killed people in deep water.

"Bottom composition?" Ryder asked, studying the depth sounder readings.

"Sand and coral rubble," Jin reported from the electronics station. "Depth varies from seventy-five to eighty-five feet. Current running north to south at maybe two knots."

"Manageable," Miguel confirmed, testing his underwater communications system. "Visibility should be good at this depth if the weather holds."

Zara watched the dive preparations with professional interest mixed with growing anxiety. Her advanced open water certification was legitimate, but watching Miguel's expert handling of technical diving equipment made her aware of how much she didn't know about deep-water operations.

"You've done wreck diving before?" Ryder asked, noticing her attention to the equipment setup.

"Some," she replied carefully. "But nothing this deep or this complex. Most of my underwater work has been in shallow water crime scene recovery."

"Crime scene recovery," Jin repeated with interest. "That's specialized training."

"Federal agents learn all kinds of weird skills," Zara said, which was true enough. "You never know when you might need to recover evidence from the bottom of a lake or river."

"Fair dinkum," Ryder said with approval. "Those skills will translate well to archaeological diving. Same attention to detail, same careful documentation procedures."

Miguel finished his equipment check and moved to the dive platform at the boat's stern. "Initial reconnaissance dive," he announced. "Twenty minutes bottom time, survey the wreck site, identify major structural features and potential hazards."

"Copy that," Ryder replied from the helm. "Jin, monitor dive communications. Tomás, maintain position over the site. Dr. Baptiste, help me spot for debris or structural hazards that might not show on sonar."

The formality of using her cover name stung a little, but Zara understood operational security. Even though the crew now knew she was federal law enforcement, maintaining some aspects of her cover identity kept things simpler for everyone involved.

Miguel entered the water with practiced ease, his bubbles trailing behind him as he descended toward the bottom. The surface of the Caribbean looked deceptively peaceful, giving no indication of the drama playing out eighty feet below.

"Contact on the bottom," Miguel's voice came through the underwater communication system, distorted by depth and electronic processing but clearly excited. "Definite wreck site, substantial debris field, metal detector showing strong returns."

"Description of the wreck," Ryder requested, his naval training taking over dive operations coordination.

"Hull section intact, maybe forty meters long," Miguel reported, his voice becoming clearer as he adjusted his communication equipment. "Broken amidships, stern section separated and lying on its side. Lots of scattered debris, but main structural elements are recognizable."

"Age and condition?" Jin asked, monitoring multiple data feeds from Miguel's equipment.

"Consistent with nineteenth-century merchant vessel construction," Miguel replied. "Iron fastenings, copper sheathing on the hull, design elements that match Spanish colonial period shipping."

Zara felt excitement building in her chest. After six months of investigation and research, they'd actually found the *Caribbean Star*. The ship that had been carrying fifty million dollars in conflict diamonds when Hurricane Isabel sent her to the bottom of the Caribbean.

"Any sign of cargo?" Ryder asked, getting to the question they were all thinking.

"Negative on obvious cargo containers," Miguel responded. "But there's a lot of debris and structural collapse. Gonna need multiple dives and careful excavation to access interior spaces."

"Understood," Ryder said. "Complete your survey and return to surface. We'll plan detailed search operations based on your reconnaissance."

The next fifteen minutes felt like hours as they waited for Miguel to complete his initial survey of the wreck site. Jin monitored his communications and vital signs while Tomás maintained their position over the coordinates and Ryder studied charts and dive tables.

Zara found herself watching the horizon for signs of other vessels, her federal training making her paranoid about Viktor's people showing up just as they'd located their target.

"Surface," Miguel's voice announced through the communication system. "Coming up now."

The Mexican diver appeared at the surface fifty yards from the boat, his mask and regulator clearly visible as he swam back to the dive platform. Jin and Tomás helped him aboard while Ryder and Zara gathered around for the debrief.

"It's definitely the *Caribbean Star*," Miguel confirmed, pulling off his mask and shaking water from his hair. "Hull design, construction materials, location - everything matches the historical descriptions."

"Condition of the wreck?" Ryder asked.

"Better than expected for a hurricane victim," Miguel replied, accepting a bottle of water from Jin. "The ship broke apart when she sank, but the major sections are intact and accessible. Sand and coral growth, but not enough to completely obscure structural features."

"What about cargo access?" Zara asked, trying to keep the urgency out of her voice.

"That's the challenging part," Miguel said, consulting his waterproof notes. "The main cargo holds are partially collapsed and filled with sand and debris. We'll need to do careful excavation to access interior spaces without damaging artifacts or causing further structural collapse."

"Time estimate for full cargo recovery?" Ryder asked.

Miguel considered the question carefully. "With proper safety protocols and documentation? Two days minimum, maybe three if we encounter unexpected complications."

Zara's heart sank. They had maybe twelve hours before the approaching weather system made diving impossible, and Viktor's people could show up at any time with superior resources and no regard for archaeological procedures.

"What if we prioritized specific areas?" she asked. "Focused on the most likely locations for high-value cargo?"

"Possible," Miguel agreed. "Captain's cabin, strong room areas, passenger quarters where valuables might have been stored. We could concentrate on those spaces first."

"Right then," Ryder decided. "We'll do targeted recovery operations. Miguel, you take the lead on dive planning. Jin, monitor weather and communications. Tomás, maintain security watch. Dr. Baptiste, you're with me on the second dive team."

Zara felt a thrill of excitement mixed with terror. She was actually going to dive on the *Caribbean Star*, search for the evidence that could make or break her investigation.

"My diving experience is limited," she reminded them. "I don't want to be a liability on deep-water operations."

"You'll be fine," Ryder assured her with a confidence that made her pulse quicken. "I'll be your dive buddy, and Miguel will guide us to the most promising areas. Your job is to help identify and document potential evidence."

The next hour was spent in intensive dive planning and equipment preparation. Zara struggled into a wetsuit that clung to her curves in ways that made Ryder's eyes darken with appreciation, then learned to use the boat's professional diving equipment.

The rebreather system was more complex than the standard scuba gear she'd trained with, but Jin's patient technical instruction and Miguel's practical tips helped her understand the basics. The underwater metal detector would be her primary tool, scanning for metallic objects that might indicate diamond storage containers.

"Remember," Ryder said as they prepared to enter the water, "diamonds don't register on metal detectors. We're looking for containers, safes, strong boxes, anything that might have been used to transport valuable cargo."

"Got it," Zara replied, testing her underwater communication system. "Look for the boxes, not the rocks inside them."

"Exactly," Miguel confirmed. "And stay close to Ryder. Wreck diving can be dangerous if you don't know what you're doing."

The water was crystal clear and surprisingly warm as they descended toward the bottom. Zara's ears popped as they went deeper, and she had to work to equalize the pressure. But the view was incredible - tropical fish scattered like jewels through the water column, coral formations creating underwater gardens, and far below, the dark shadow of the *Caribbean Star* taking shape on the sandy bottom.

"First wreck dive?" Ryder's voice came through her headset, distorted by water and electronics but warmly familiar.

"Yeah," she replied, trying to keep the nervousness out of her voice. "It's beautiful and terrifying at the same time."

"Fair dinkum, that's exactly right," he agreed with a laugh. "Beauty and danger - that's what makes it addictive."

As they approached the wreck, Zara could make out details that Miguel's description hadn't fully conveyed. The *Caribbean Star* was huge, her hull sections dwarfing the divers as they swam along her broken length. Coral and marine growth covered much of the structure, but the basic ship design was clearly visible.

"There," Miguel's voice directed them toward the stern section. "Captain's quarters should be in that area, and that's where valuable cargo was usually stored."

They swam through what had once been elegant passenger spaces, now filled with sand and inhabited by tropical fish. Zara's metal detector began chirping as they entered what looked like a collapsed cabin area.

"Strong return," she reported, following the electronic signals toward a pile of debris near what might have been a built-in safe or strong room.

"Careful," Ryder warned, his hand touching her shoulder as she moved closer to the debris pile. "Structural collapse can shift without warning."

Working together, they began carefully moving pieces of wreckage and coral growth away from the metal detector's target area. The work was slow and methodical, with constant attention to safety and documentation.

After twenty minutes of excavation, Jin's voice came through their headsets with urgency that made Zara's blood run cold.

"Multiple contacts on surface radar," she reported. "Three fast boats approaching from the northeast, high speed, military formation."

Viktor's people. They'd found the *Caribbean Star* site.

"Time to surface?" Miguel asked, already beginning to pack up his equipment.

"Five minutes," Ryder replied calmly, though Zara could hear the tension in his voice. "Whatever we're gonna find, we need to find it now."

Zara attacked the debris pile with desperate energy, her metal detector screaming as she got closer to whatever was buried in the sand and coral. Her hands found something hard and metallic, rectangular in shape, about the size of a small briefcase.

"Got something," she announced, working to free the object from decades of marine growth.

"What is it?" Ryder asked, moving to help her.

The object came free suddenly, and Zara found herself holding a corroded but intact metal case with brass fittings and what looked like the remnants of a locking mechanism.

"Document case," Miguel identified, examining the artifact quickly. "Watertight construction, designed to protect papers or small valuable items."

"Surface, now," Jin's voice cut through their excitement. "Those boats are closing fast, and they're not responding to radio calls."

The ascent to the surface felt like it took hours, though Zara knew it was only minutes. Her heart pounded with adrenaline as they rose through the blue water, the metal case clutched protectively against her chest.

They broke the surface to find the *Siren's Call* already moving, engines at full power as Ryder's crew prepared for another high-speed pursuit. The three approaching boats were clearly visible now, sleek and fast and bristling with armed personnel.

"Same boats from Nassau," Tomás confirmed as they climbed aboard. "Viktor's people, no question."

"Can we outrun them?" Zara asked, stripping off her diving equipment while the boat accelerated.

"Not for long," Ryder replied grimly. "But we might not have to. Look at those clouds."

The weather system Tomás had been tracking was building faster than predicted, with dark storm clouds forming on the northern horizon. Lightning flickered in the distance, and the wind was already starting to pick up.

"Storm's moving faster than forecast," Tomás confirmed. "We're about to get hit with some serious weather."

"Good," Ryder said with grim satisfaction. "Viktor's people might have faster boats, but they don't know these waters like we do. Storm conditions will level the playing field."

As if summoned by his words, the first gunshots rang out across the water. Viktor's lead boat was close enough now that Zara could see individual gunmen taking aim at the *Siren's Call*.

"Here we go again," Miguel muttered, securing diving equipment while bullets whistled overhead.

But this time, they had something Viktor wanted desperately - physical evidence from the *Caribbean Star*, potentially including documents or artifacts that could expose the entire diamond trafficking operation.

The corroded metal case sat on the deck between them, its contents unknown but possibly worth fifty million dollars and several lives.

Time to find out what secrets the Caribbean had been keeping.

The storm was coming, Viktor's people were closing in, and somewhere in the metal case was evidence that could change everything.

Zara gripped the artifact tighter as the *Siren's Call* raced toward an uncertain destiny, carrying secrets from the past that might determine the future.

CHAPTER FIVE

The corroded metal case sat on the *Siren's Call's* deck like a time bomb, its brass fittings green with decades of salt water but the locking mechanism still intact. Zara knelt beside it while bullets whistled overhead, her hands shaking with adrenaline as she worked to open the case that might contain fifty million dollars worth of evidence.

"Can you get it open?" Ryder shouted from the helm, pushing the engines to maximum power as Viktor's boats closed the distance behind them. The Australian's knuckles were white on the wheel, his green eyes focused on the navigation displays showing coral reefs and shallow water ahead.

"Working on it," Zara replied, her Miami street knowledge kicking in as she examined the corroded lock mechanism. Growing up in Little Haiti had taught her things federal training never covered, including how to open locks when you didn't have the key. "Give me thirty seconds."

More gunfire erupted from the pursuing boats, automatic weapons fire stitching a line of foam across their wake. The bullets were getting closer, and Viktor's people were obviously done with warning shots.

"Thirty seconds we might not have," Miguel called from the stern, where he was securing diving equipment while keeping watch on their pursuers. "Those boats are gaining fast."

The lock mechanism was corroded but not destroyed. Zara pulled a dive knife from her equipment belt and worked the blade into the mechanism, applying pressure and leverage in ways Uncle Ronny had taught her for dealing with rusted boat hardware.

"*Vamos, maldita cosa*," she muttered in Spanish, her cultural background sliding into the words as stress made her code-switch between languages. "Come on, you piece of shit."

The lock gave way with a metallic click, and the case opened to reveal its contents. Inside, wrapped in what had once been oiled canvas but was now just soggy decay, were several items that made Zara's heart race with excitement.

Documents. Photographs. And a small leather pouch that felt heavy with promise.

"What you got?" Ryder asked, glancing back from the helm while navigating around a coral head that could tear their hull open.

"Jackpot," Zara replied, carefully lifting the leather pouch from the case. The weight and feel suggested gemstones, and when she loosened the drawstring, diamonds spilled into her palm like captured starlight.

"Jesus fucking Christ," Miguel breathed, abandoning his watch duties to stare at the stones. "Are those real?"

"Real as it gets," Zara confirmed, studying the diamonds with her federal training in contraband identification. "These are uncut conflict diamonds, probably worth millions. And look at this."

She held up one of the documents that had survived decades underwater thanks to the waterproof case. It was a shipping manifest, written in Spanish, but listing cargo that didn't match the official records they'd studied.

"Private cargo manifest," Jin observed, taking a quick look while monitoring radar and communications. "Someone was keeping very careful records of what they were really carrying."

"And this," Zara added, holding up a photograph that made her blood run cold. The black and white image showed two men shaking hands beside a ship that looked very much like the *Caribbean Star*. One man was clearly Spanish colonial period, but the other...

"Bloody hell," Ryder said, recognizing the implications immediately. "That's contemporary clothing. This photo was taken recently, not during the colonial period."

"Someone's been using the *Caribbean Star* wreck as a drop site," Zara realized, the pieces clicking together in her mind. "These diamonds aren't historical artifacts. They're contemporary contraband that was being stored in the wreck until it could be safely recovered."

The implications were staggering. The *Caribbean Star* hadn't just been carrying diamonds when she sank - she'd been used as an underwater storage facility for ongoing diamond trafficking operations. Which meant Viktor's people weren't just trying to recover historical evidence.

They were trying to recover active criminal assets worth fifty million dollars.

"That's why they're so bloody desperate," Ryder said with grim understanding. "It's not just about covering up old crimes. It's about protecting current operations."

"And that's why Martinez has been feeding them information," Zara added, her federal training connecting the dots. "She's not just covering up past corruption. She's actively participating in ongoing criminal operations."

A new burst of gunfire, closer than before, reminded them that philosophical discussions about federal corruption would have to wait. Viktor's boats were less than a quarter mile behind and closing fast.

"Storm's building faster," Tomás announced from the weather station, studying satellite imagery that showed the approaching system intensifying. "We got maybe twenty minutes before conditions become too rough for safe boat operations."

"Can we use that?" Zara asked, securing the diamonds and documents in her waterproof evidence bag.

"Damn right we can," Ryder replied with the kind of grin that had probably gotten him in trouble during his naval service. "Viktor's people might have faster boats, but they don't know these waters in storm conditions."

He swung the *Siren's Call* hard to port, heading toward a reef system that showed on his charts as a maze of coral heads and shallow passages. The kind of water that required local knowledge and balls of steel to navigate safely.

"You sure about this?" Miguel asked, watching their depth sounder readings drop toward dangerously shallow water.

"Sure as death and taxes," Ryder confirmed, his Australian accent thick with concentration. "These reefs will either save us or kill us, but Viktor's people won't be able to follow."

The first drops of rain began hitting the deck as they entered the reef system, and the wind was picking up enough to create whitecaps on the previously calm Caribbean water. The approaching storm was moving faster than anyone had predicted.

Behind them, Viktor's lead boat was hesitating at the edge of the reef system, clearly uncertain about following them into water that could destroy their hull with one navigation error.

"They're slowing down," Jin reported with satisfaction. "Probably trying to decide if it's worth the risk."

"It's not," Ryder said confidently, threading their boat through a passage barely wider than their beam. "Not in these conditions, not without local knowledge."

But as they emerged from the reef passage into deeper water, a new threat appeared on the horizon. A helicopter, military-style, approaching fast from the northeast.

"Viktor's air support," Miguel identified, shading his eyes against the strengthening wind. "That's a serious aircraft, military grade."

"Can we outrun it?" Zara asked, though she suspected she already knew the answer.

"Not in open water," Ryder replied grimly. "But helicopter operations become bloody dangerous in storm conditions. If we can stay ahead of them until the weather really hits..."

As if responding to his words, lightning flashed in the dark clouds building on the northern horizon, followed by thunder that rolled across the water like cannon fire. The storm was close now, close enough to taste the electricity in the air.

"There," Tomás called from the navigation station, pointing toward a cluster of small islands barely visible through the increasing rain. "Mangrove islands, shallow water, lots of channels. Helicopter won't be able to operate effectively in that terrain."

"Right then," Ryder decided, changing course toward the islands while rain began pelting the deck in earnest. "We play hide and seek in the mangroves until this weather passes."

The next hour was a nightmare of navigation through narrow channels and overhanging vegetation while tropical storm conditions built around them. The helicopter circled overhead when possible, but the increasingly violent weather made flying dangerous even for experienced military pilots.

Viktor's boats had given up the chase entirely, returning to open water rather than risk destruction in the reef systems during storm conditions. But the helicopter persisted, searching whenever the weather allowed.

"They know we found something," Jin observed, monitoring radio communications between the helicopter and what sounded like a command vessel beyond radar range. "They're coordinating a wider search pattern."

"Let them search," Ryder said, maneuvering through a particularly narrow channel between mangrove-covered islands. "We've got what we came for, and we know where to find more."

The diamonds in Zara's evidence bag represented only a small portion of what the *Caribbean Star* had been carrying. The documents suggested ongoing storage operations, which meant there had to be a main cache somewhere in the wreck.

"We need to go back," she said, voicing what they were all thinking. "These diamonds prove the trafficking operation exists, but we need the main cache to have enough evidence to bring down the entire network."

"Back to the wreck site?" Miguel asked with concern. "In these conditions?"

"Storm will pass," Tomás said, studying his weather data. "Maybe six hours, then we'll have a window before the next system moves through."

"Viktor's people will be waiting," Jin pointed out. "They know we found the site now. They'll have boats positioned around the coordinates."

"Then we don't approach from the obvious direction," Ryder said with tactical thinking. "We come in from the south, use the storm's aftermath to mask our approach, dive fast and get out before they realize we're there."

It was dangerous, possibly suicidal, but it was also their best chance to recover enough evidence to expose the entire diamond trafficking network and clear Marcus MacCallum's name.

The afternoon wore on with tropical storm intensity, rain hammering the boat's superstructure while wind howled through the mangrove channels. They took shelter in a deep cove surrounded by overhanging vegetation, hidden from aerial search while they rode out the worst of the weather.

During the storm, Zara worked on documenting their discoveries. The diamonds, documents, and photographs from the metal case painted a picture of systematic criminal activity spanning decades. The *Caribbean Star* had been used as an underwater storage facility, with periodic recovery operations moving conflict diamonds through Caribbean shipping routes to international markets.

"This is bigger than we thought," she told Ryder as they studied the evidence together in the boat's main cabin. The storm raged outside, but inside they were dry and safe, working by the light of battery-powered lamps.

"How big?" he asked, his green eyes serious as he examined the Spanish shipping documents.

"International syndicate big," Zara replied, her federal training recognizing the scope of the operation. "Multiple countries, government officials, probably military personnel. This isn't just Viktor's operation - he's part of something much larger."

"And your handler Martinez is connected to all of it."

"Has to be," Zara confirmed. "The level of protection this operation has received, the inside information they've had access to - it requires corruption at the highest levels of federal law enforcement."

Ryder was quiet for a long moment, processing the implications.

"If we expose this," he said finally, "it's gonna bring down a lot of powerful people. People who won't hesitate to kill anyone who threatens them."

"I know," Zara replied simply. "But it's also gonna clear your brother's name and put war criminals in prison where they belong."

"Worth the risk?"

She looked at him across the small table, this man who'd risked everything to help her mission, who'd made love to her like she was the most precious thing in his world, who was willing to dive back into danger to seek justice for his dead brother.

"Worth any risk," she said with certainty.

The storm began to weaken around sunset, wind dropping from hurricane force to merely dangerous, rain changing from torrential to merely heavy. Tomás's weather analysis suggested they'd have a six-hour window of relatively calm conditions before the next system moved through.

"Time to move," Ryder announced, firing up the engines while his crew prepared for night operations. "We hit the wreck site fast, recover the main diamond cache, and get out before Viktor's people know we're there."

"And if they're already there waiting?" Miguel asked.

"Then we improvise," Ryder replied with the kind of confidence that had made him an effective naval officer. "Wouldn't be the first time."

The run back to the *Caribbean Star* coordinates took two hours of careful navigation through post-storm conditions. Debris from the weather system floated everywhere - palm fronds, pieces of boats, even parts of buildings torn loose by hurricane-force winds.

But the chaos also provided excellent cover for their approach. Viktor's people would be dealing with their own storm damage and probably wouldn't expect immediate return to the wreck site.

"Contact," Jin reported as they approached the coordinates. "One vessel holding position over the site, maybe a hundred meters off our target."

"Just one?" Ryder asked with surprise. "That's either overconfidence or they're short on resources."

"Could be a trap," Zara warned, her federal training making her paranoid about easy targets.

"Could be," Ryder agreed. "But we won't know until we get closer."

The single vessel turned out to be a large motor yacht, probably Viktor's command ship, anchored directly over the

Caribbean Star wreck site. Lights blazed from her superstructure, and armed figures were visible on deck.

"They're running dive operations," Miguel observed, studying the vessel through binoculars. "Dive platform set up, underwater lights deployed, the whole nine yards."

"Bastards are trying to beat us to the main cache," Ryder said with grim anger.

"Then we stop them," Zara said simply. "Whatever it takes."

The approach to the wreck site required all of Ryder's naval training and local knowledge. They came in dark and silent, using post-storm conditions to mask their movements while positioning for a surprise assault on Viktor's diving operation.

"Two divers in the water," Jin reported, monitoring underwater communications. "They've found something big down there."

"Main diamond cache," Miguel confirmed, watching through night vision equipment. "They're bringing up cases, lots of them."

Fifty million dollars in conflict diamonds, enough evidence to expose an international criminal network, being stolen by the very people they were trying to prosecute.

"Like hell," Zara said, her Miami street attitude overriding federal protocols. "Those diamonds are evidence in a federal investigation."

"Fair dinkum," Ryder agreed with a predatory smile. "Time to remind Viktor's people that piracy has consequences."

The *Siren's Call* emerged from the darkness like an avenging ghost, engines at full power as they approached Viktor's command vessel. The element of surprise lasted exactly long enough for them to get within boarding range.

Then all hell broke loose.

Automatic weapons fire erupted from Viktor's yacht, muzzle flashes lighting up the Caribbean night as professional mercenaries responded to the surprise attack. But Ryder's naval training and his crew's maritime experience made them formidable opponents even against superior firepower.

"Miguel, prepare to board," Ryder commanded, maneuvering alongside the larger vessel with precision that spoke to years of military experience. "Jin, maintain communications and engine readiness. Tomás, cover our approach."

"What about me?" Zara asked, checking her sidearm and federal equipment.

"You're with me," Ryder said with a grin that was equal parts excitement and determination. "Time to recover some evidence, Agent Baptiste."

The boarding action was swift and violent, two desperate groups fighting for control of diamonds that could change the course of international criminal justice. Viktor's mercenaries had superior numbers and firepower, but Ryder's team had surprise, superior training, and the kind of motivation that came from seeking justice rather than profit.

The battle raged across the yacht's deck while underwater, Viktor's divers continued their recovery operations, probably unaware of the surface combat that would determine whether their efforts served criminal enterprise or law enforcement.

Zara found herself in close-quarters combat with professional killers, her federal training and street instincts combining to keep her alive while she fought toward the dive platform where cases of diamonds were being brought up from the *Caribbean Star*.

"The diamonds!" she shouted to Ryder, who was engaged in hand-to-hand combat with two mercenaries near the yacht's wheelhouse. "They're bringing up the main cache!"

"Go!" he replied, disabling one opponent with a technique that definitely hadn't come from treasure hunting manuals. "Secure the evidence!"

Zara reached the dive platform just as Viktor's divers surfaced with another case of diamonds. Without hesitation, she dove into the Caribbean water, her federal training in water operations taking over as she swam toward the underwater lights marking the *Caribbean Star* wreck.

The scene at the bottom was surreal - the broken Spanish merchant vessel illuminated by powerful dive lights while professional criminals systematically looted the cargo that could expose their entire network. Cases of diamonds were stacked near the wreck like underwater treasure, waiting to be lifted to the surface.

But not if Zara had anything to say about it.

She swam toward the main cache, her federal training in underwater operations serving her well as she navigated the complex terrain of the wreck site. Viktor's divers were focused on their work, not expecting interference from a federal agent with advanced water rescue certification.

The confrontation that followed was unlike anything in her law enforcement experience - underwater combat for control of evidence that could bring down an international criminal network. No backup, no support, just her training and determination against professional criminals who would kill her without hesitation if they got the chance.

But Zara Baptiste had grown up in Miami waters, learned to swim in Biscayne Bay, been trained by Uncle Ronny to respect the ocean and use it as an ally. The Caribbean was her element as much as the criminals', and she had advantages they didn't expect.

The battle for the diamonds had moved underwater, where federal training and cultural background would determine whether justice or corruption prevailed.

Time to find out what the ocean had decided.

Eighty feet underwater, fighting for your life while trying to secure federal evidence, was not covered in DEA training manuals. But Uncle Ronny's lessons about Caribbean water came flooding back as Zara faced off against Viktor's professional divers in the underwater cathedral of the *Caribbean Star* wreck.

The first diver came at her with a dive knife, his movements clumsy in the water despite obvious combat training. Land fighters always struggled with three-dimensional underwater combat, and Zara used that advantage, twisting away from his thrust and using his momentum to send him tumbling into the wreck's collapsed superstructure.

The second diver was smarter, keeping distance while trying to signal the surface team. But Zara's federal water rescue training included underwater combat scenarios, and she closed the distance fast, using a technique that would have made her defensive tactics instructors proud.

Her dive knife found the air hose connecting his breathing apparatus to his tank. Not a killing blow, but enough to send him racing for the surface before he drowned eighty feet down.

That left her alone with the diamond cache and about ten minutes of air in her emergency tank.

The cases were heavy, designed for secure transport of valuable cargo. Each one probably contained millions of dollars in uncut conflict diamonds, evidence of war crimes and international corruption that reached into the highest levels of government.

She couldn't carry them all to the surface, but she could make sure Viktor's people couldn't recover them either.

Working fast, Zara began dragging the diamond cases deeper into the *Caribbean Star's* broken hull, hiding them in collapsed sections where recovery would require major excavation efforts. Each case contained millions of dollars in uncut conflict diamonds - the main cache that, combined with the ten million she'd already recovered, represented the full fifty-million-dollar theft from federal custody. It wasn't perfect, but it would buy time for legitimate federal backup to arrive.

If legitimate federal backup existed anymore. With Martinez compromised and the investigation blown, Zara wasn't sure who she could trust in her own agency.

Her air gauge was showing red when she finally started her ascent, following proper decompression procedures despite the urgent situation on the surface. Nitrogen narcosis and decompression sickness could kill her just as dead as Viktor's bullets.

The surface broke around her like emerging from another world. The yacht battle was still raging, automatic weapons fire and shouted commands in multiple languages creating chaos on the Caribbean night. But the *Siren's Call* was holding her own, Ryder's naval training and his crew's determination proving equal to professional mercenaries.

"Zara!" Ryder's voice carried across the water as she surfaced near the dive platform. "You all right, love?"

"Diamonds are secured," she called back, swimming toward the platform while gunfire crackled overhead. "Hidden in the wreck where they can't recover them easily."

"Right then," Ryder replied with satisfaction. "Time to finish this."

The final assault on Viktor's command yacht was coordinated chaos. Miguel's commercial diving experience made him deadly in close quarters, Jin's technical expertise allowed her to disable the yacht's communications and navigation systems, and Tomás's decades of Caribbean seamanship let him position the *Siren's Call* for maximum tactical advantage.

But it was Ryder's naval combat training that turned the tide. Moving through Viktor's mercenaries like a force of nature, the Australian captain systematically eliminated threats while working toward the yacht's bridge where the operation's commanders were coordinating the diamond recovery.

Zara fought her way to the dive platform, securing the cases that had already been brought up while preventing further recovery operations. Federal evidence protocols required chain of custody documentation, but staying alive took priority over paperwork.

The battle climax came when Viktor Kozlov himself appeared on the yacht's bridge, a tall man with dead eyes and the kind of casual cruelty that came from years of profiting from human misery. He carried an assault rifle like he knew how to use it, and the look he gave Zara suggested personal interest in her death.

"Agent Zara Baptiste," he called out in Russian-accented English, his voice carrying over the gunfire and engine noise. "You have caused me considerable inconvenience."

"You ain't seen nothing yet, *papi*," Zara replied, her Miami attitude overriding federal protocols as she faced down an international war criminal. "This is for every person your blood diamonds killed."

The firefight that followed was intense and personal. Viktor's people had superior firepower, but Ryder's team had better training and motivation that came from seeking justice rather than protecting criminal profits.

When the smoke cleared, Viktor's yacht was disabled, his mercenaries were either dead or surrendering, and the Russian arms dealer himself was wounded but alive - perfect for federal prosecution if Zara could get him back to legitimate authorities.

"Well, that was bloody exciting," Ryder said with characteristic Australian understatement as they secured their prisoners and evidence. "Remind me why we didn't just call the Coast Guard?"

"Because my handler's corrupt, my agency's been compromised, and the only people I trust are standing on this deck," Zara replied honestly. "We're on our own until we can figure out who's really working for justice."

The diamond cases recovered from the surface contained exactly what the documents had suggested - millions of dollars in conflict diamonds that had been stored in the *Caribbean Star* wreck for periodic recovery and transport to international markets. Each stone was evidence of war crimes, corruption, and human suffering that reached into the highest levels of government.

"This is enough to bring down the entire network," Zara said, documenting the evidence with her federal equipment. "Viktor, Martinez, everyone connected to the trafficking operation."

"Including proof of Marcus's innocence," Ryder added, studying shipping documents that clearly showed the timeline of diamond theft and storage. "These records prove he was framed by the same people who've been using the wreck for criminal operations."

Need You Now

The emotional weight of vindication for his dead brother was written across Ryder's weathered features. Six months of grief and anger finally had a target, and the evidence to achieve justice.

But their celebration was interrupted by Jin's urgent voice from the communications station.

"Multiple contacts approaching," she reported. "Fast boats, helicopter support, military formation. This time it's not Viktor's people."

The radar screen showed a coordinated assault force approaching from multiple directions - the kind of response that suggested serious government backing.

"Coast Guard?" Miguel asked hopefully.

"Wrong configuration," Jin replied, studying the electronic signatures. "These are military vessels, not law enforcement."

Zara's blood ran cold as she realized what was happening. Martinez hadn't just compromised her investigation - she'd arranged for military intervention to eliminate witnesses and recover the diamonds for the criminal network.

"They're not here to rescue us," she said with growing horror. "They're here to kill us and recover the evidence."

"Fair dinkum," Ryder said with grim understanding. "Your corrupt handler called in favors from corrupt military contacts."

The approaching force was overwhelming - multiple fast attack craft, helicopter gunships, probably special operations personnel with authorization to eliminate all witnesses to preserve operational security.

"We can't fight that," Miguel said, studying the approaching armada through binoculars. "Not with what we've got."

"Then we don't fight," Zara decided, her federal training shifting to survival mode. "We disappear."

"Disappear where?" Jin asked. "We're in the middle of the Caribbean with nowhere to hide."

Zara looked at the cases of diamond evidence, then at the disabled yacht where Viktor and his surviving mercenaries were secured as prisoners. The evidence they'd recovered could expose international corruption and clear Marcus MacCallum's name, but only if they survived long enough to deliver it to legitimate authorities.

"The diamonds go back down," she decided. "Hidden in the wreck where we can recover them later. Viktor comes with us as proof of the criminal network. And we use the storm system approaching from the west to cover our escape."

"Back into storm conditions?" Tomás asked with concern. "That western system is showing Category 2 hurricane development."

"Better than facing military assassins with unlimited resources," Zara pointed out. "Storms are dangerous, but they're not deliberately trying to kill us."

The plan was desperate but potentially workable. The second storm system would provide cover for escape while making pursuit operations dangerous for even military vessels. If they could stay ahead of the weather and find somewhere to hide until legitimate federal backup could be arranged...

"Right then," Ryder decided. "We send the diamonds back to Davy Jones, keep Viktor as our insurance policy, and run for our bloody lives."

The next thirty minutes were controlled chaos as they prepared for emergency departure. The diamond cases went back underwater, hidden in new locations within the *Caribbean Star* wreck that only they would know. Viktor was transferred to the *Siren's Call* as a prisoner, wounded but valuable for his knowledge of the criminal network.

The approaching military force was less than ten miles away when they abandoned Viktor's disabled yacht and ran for the storm system building on the western horizon.

"This is insane," Miguel observed as they headed directly toward hurricane conditions while military vessels pursued them across increasingly rough seas.

"Insane is the only option we got left," Zara replied, securing evidence and equipment while tropical storm winds began buffeting their boat. "Sometimes you gotta choose between dangerous and deadly."

The chase that followed was unlike anything in maritime history - federal agents and treasure hunters running from corrupt military forces through the leading edge of a Caribbean hurricane, carrying evidence that could expose international criminal networks reaching to the highest levels of government.

Lightning crackled overhead while forty-foot waves tossed their boat like a toy. The military pursuit force was larger and better equipped, but they were also less willing to risk everything in storm conditions that could kill professional sailors.

"They're falling back," Jin reported, monitoring radar contacts through the storm interference. "Military discipline - they won't risk their vessels and personnel for a pursuit operation."

"But they'll be waiting when we come out of the storm," Ryder pointed out, fighting the helm as another massive wave broke over their bow.

"Then we don't come out where they expect," Zara said, studying charts of the Caribbean while their boat pitched and rolled through hurricane seas. "We disappear completely until we can arrange legitimate federal contact."

The storm raged around them for six hours, testing every aspect of their seamanship and survival skills. But when dawn broke over calmer seas, the *Siren's Call* and her crew were still alive, still carrying evidence that could change everything.

Viktor sat in the main cabin, secured but conscious, his dead eyes studying his captors with the kind of calculation that suggested he wasn't finished causing trouble.

"You cannot hide forever," he said in his Russian-accented English. "My associates will find you, and when they do, your deaths will serve as examples to others who interfere with our operations."

"We'll see about that," Zara replied, checking her federal communication equipment for signs of legitimate contact. "Right now, you're our prisoner, and that evidence is gonna put you away forever."

But Viktor's smile suggested he knew something they didn't, and the look in his eyes made it clear that the battle for justice was far from over.

The Caribbean stretched endlessly around them, beautiful and dangerous, keeping its secrets while new ones were created. They had evidence, they had a prisoner, and they had each other.

Time to find out if that would be enough to expose international corruption and clear the name of a dead hero.

The ocean held all the answers, waiting for someone brave enough to dive deep and bring them to light.

CHAPTER SIX

The morning sun painted the Caribbean in shades of gold and turquoise, but Zara couldn't enjoy the beauty. The *Siren's Call* drifted in calm water fifty miles from the *Caribbean Star* wreck site, hidden among a cluster of uninhabited islands while they figured out their next move. Viktor sat tied up in the main cabin, his dead eyes watching everything, waiting for his chance.

But right now, Zara's attention was focused on Ryder's injured shoulder.

The wound had seemed minor during the firefight on Viktor's yacht - just a graze from a ricocheted bullet that had torn through his shirt and left a bloody furrow across his left shoulder blade. But now, twelve hours later, the injury was looking infected and Ryder was showing signs of fever.

"Let me see," Zara said, helping him remove his shirt in the boat's small medical station. Her federal training included combat medic certification, and what she saw made her stomach clench with worry.

The bullet graze was deeper than it had first appeared, with ragged edges that hadn't been properly cleaned during the chaos of their escape. Worse, the skin around the wound was hot and red, with the kind of angry inflammation that meant serious infection.

"Looks like shit, doesn't it?" Ryder asked, trying to make light of the situation despite the pain obvious in his green eyes.

"Yeah, it does," Zara replied honestly, her Miami street background making her direct about medical realities. "You got an infection going, and it's spreading fast. When's the last time you had antibiotics?"

"Can't remember," he admitted, wincing as she examined the wound more closely. "Been a while since I needed them."

That was the problem with operating outside official channels - no access to proper medical care, no backup when things went wrong, no safety net except what they could provide for themselves.

"I can clean and dress the wound," she said, gathering medical supplies from the boat's first aid kit. "But you need real antibiotics, not just antiseptic and bandages."

"We can't exactly pull into Nassau General Hospital," Ryder pointed out. "Viktor's people probably have half the medical facilities in the Caribbean watching for us."

He was right, but that didn't make the medical reality any less dangerous. Without proper treatment, the infection could spread into his bloodstream, causing sepsis and potentially death. Zara had seen gunshot wound infections kill strong men in Miami, and she wasn't about to lose Ryder to something preventable.

"I got some emergency antibiotics in my federal kit," she said, remembering the medical supplies she'd packed for the undercover operation. "Military grade stuff, should knock out the infection if we catch it early enough."

"You sure about that?" Miguel asked from the doorway, concern evident in his voice. "Infections from gunshot wounds can be tricky."

"I'm sure," Zara replied with more confidence than she felt. "I've treated worse in the field."

The next hour was spent cleaning Ryder's wound with careful attention to removing all debris and damaged tissue. The work was painful for him and difficult for her, but necessary to prevent the infection from spreading further.

"Fucking hell," he muttered through gritted teeth as she irrigated the deepest part of the wound channel. "That hurts worse than getting shot."

"Good," Zara said, her concentration absolute as she worked. "Pain means nerve function is intact. It's when gunshot wounds stop hurting that you worry."

Her hands were steady and competent as she cleaned and dressed the injury, federal medical training combining with cultural knowledge from growing up in a community where people often couldn't afford proper healthcare. Uncle Ronny had taught all his nieces and nephews basic medical care, because sometimes the ocean hurt people far from hospitals.

"There," she said finally, securing the last piece of medical tape. "Clean, dressed, and loaded with enough antibiotics to kill anything short of flesh-eating bacteria."

"You're a bloody miracle worker," Ryder said, testing his shoulder's range of motion carefully. "Feels better already."

"Give it six hours for the antibiotics to kick in," she advised. "And don't do anything stupid that might reopen the wound."

"Define stupid," he said with a slight grin that made her pulse quicken despite the medical circumstances.

"Getting into firefights with international criminals," she replied, matching his smile. "At least for the next few days."

The tender moment was interrupted by Jin's urgent voice from the communications station.

"Incoming call on federal emergency frequency," she announced. "Someone's trying to reach Agent Baptiste directly."

Zara's blood went cold. Her emergency communication protocols were known only to her immediate supervisors in the DEA, which meant either legitimate backup had finally arrived or her corrupt handler was making contact.

"Put it through," she said, moving to the communications equipment while Ryder stayed in the medical station to rest.

Agent Sarah Martinez's voice came through the encrypted channel with crystal clarity, sounding exactly like the concerned federal supervisor she was supposed to be.

"Agent Baptiste, thank God," Martinez said, relief evident in her voice. "We've been trying to reach you for hours. What's your status?"

"Alive and operational," Zara replied carefully, not revealing their location or the evidence they'd recovered. "The *Deep Explorer* was sabotaged, but I survived and made contact with local assets."

"Local assets," Martinez repeated. "You mean the treasure hunters who pulled you out of the water?"

The fact that Martinez knew about Ryder and his crew was telling. Either she had legitimate intelligence sources, or she'd been monitoring the situation much more closely than a normal handler would.

"That's correct," Zara confirmed. "Captain MacCallum and his crew have been providing support for the mission."

"Agent Baptiste, I need you to listen very carefully," Martinez continued, her voice taking on the tone of superior giving critical instructions. "The situation has become extremely complex. There are multiple agencies involved now, including military intelligence and international law enforcement."

"What kind of military intelligence?" Zara asked, remembering the military vessels that had pursued them through the storm.

"The kind that doesn't appreciate federal agents operating independently in international waters," Martinez replied. "You need to come in immediately, through official channels, with proper coordination."

"Come in where?" Zara pressed. "The last I heard, our operational security was compromised."

"Nassau Coast Guard station," Martinez said immediately. "Full federal backup, proper medical support, debriefing facilities. We've cleared the security issues."

Every instinct Zara had developed in eight years of federal law enforcement was screaming warnings. Martinez was pushing too hard, offering solutions that were too convenient, trying to control the situation in ways that didn't match legitimate federal protocols.

"I need to discuss this with my local assets," Zara said carefully. "Operational security requires coordination with all personnel involved."

"Agent Baptiste," Martinez's voice sharpened with authority. "This is not a negotiation. You are a federal agent operating under my direct supervision, and I am ordering you to report to Nassau Coast Guard station immediately."

The mask was slipping. Legitimate federal supervisors didn't give ultimatums to agents in active field operations, especially when those operations had uncovered evidence of major criminal activity.

"I understand your concerns," Zara replied, stalling for time while she processed the implications. "But I need to secure the evidence we've recovered before exposing our position."

"What evidence?" Martinez asked quickly, too quickly.

"Documents, photographs, physical samples," Zara said vaguely. "Everything needed to support the investigation."

The silence that followed was telling. Martinez was calculating, trying to determine how much Zara knew and how much of a threat she represented to the criminal network.

"Agent Baptiste," Martinez finally said, her voice carrying false concern. "I'm worried about your judgment. You've been under extreme stress, operating without backup, possibly suffering from trauma-related decision-making impairment."

The psychological manipulation was textbook - undermining the agent's confidence while positioning the handler as the voice of reason and authority. Zara had seen the technique used on other agents, but experiencing it personally was infuriating.

"My judgment is fine," she replied firmly. "And my evidence is solid."

"Evidence of what, exactly?" Martinez pressed.

"Evidence that someone in federal law enforcement has been feeding information to international criminals," Zara said, watching for Martinez's reaction even though they were communicating by radio.

The pause was minimal, but telling.

"That's a serious accusation," Martinez said carefully. "Do you have specific suspects?"

"I got theories," Zara replied, her Miami accent thickening as she allowed her street attitude to slide into her voice. "And I got evidence to back them up."

"Agent Baptiste, you're starting to sound paranoid," Martinez said with the tone of a concerned supervisor dealing with an unstable subordinate. "Isolation and stress can cause federal agents to develop conspiracy theories that seem logical but aren't based in reality."

"What's not based in reality is thinking I'm stupid enough to fall for this bullshit," Zara snapped, her patience finally exhausted. "I know you're dirty, Martinez. I know you've been feeding information to Viktor's people. And I know you arranged for military intervention to eliminate witnesses."

The silence that followed was longer this time, and when Martinez spoke again, her voice had changed completely. The false concern was gone, replaced by cold professionalism.

"You always were too smart for your own good, Baptiste," she said. "That's what makes you dangerous."

"Not smart enough to figure out my own handler was selling out federal investigations," Zara replied bitterly. "How long have you been working for Viktor?"

"Three years," Martinez said with casual indifference. "Ever since my daughter's medical bills got too expensive for a federal salary to cover. Childhood leukemia is very costly, even with government health insurance."

The personal information was probably meant to generate sympathy, but it only made Zara angrier. Using a sick child to justify betraying federal investigations and getting agents killed was beyond contempt.

"So you decided to help war criminals traffic blood diamonds," she said.

"I decided to take care of my family," Martinez corrected. "Viktor's organization pays very well for information and operational support."

"And when Marcus MacCallum got too close to the truth?"

"Military diving accidents happen," Martinez said with chilling indifference. "Especially when divers are under stress from false accusations and career destruction."

The casual admission of murder made Zara's blood boil. Marcus MacCallum had been killed by his own government, framed and murdered by the very system he'd sworn to serve.

"You destroyed an innocent man and his family for money," she said, her voice tight with rage.

"I protected my family and a very profitable operation," Martinez corrected. "Marcus MacCallum was collateral damage in a much larger enterprise."

"Not anymore," Zara said firmly. "I got evidence that proves his innocence and your guilt."

"Evidence that will never see the inside of a courtroom," Martinez replied with confidence. "You're in international waters, cut off from legitimate support, hunted by military forces with authorization to eliminate security threats."

"We'll see about that."

"Yes, we will," Martinez agreed. "Because I'm looking at satellite imagery showing your exact position, and Viktor's replacement team is already en route."

Zara's blood went cold. If Martinez had satellite surveillance, their hidden position among the uninhabited islands was compromised.

"How long?" she asked, already moving to alert the crew.

"Two hours," Martinez said with satisfaction. "Professional military contractors, heavy weapons, authorization to eliminate all witnesses. You should have taken the deal to come in through official channels."

The radio went dead, leaving Zara staring at the communication equipment while her mind raced through tactical options.

"What's the situation?" Ryder asked, appearing in the doorway despite his injury and medication.

"Martinez is the mole," Zara said quickly. "She's been working with Viktor for years. And she's got military contractors heading our way with orders to kill everyone and recover the evidence."

"Bloody hell," Ryder said, his fever-bright eyes focusing with naval intensity despite his medical condition. "Time frame?"

"Two hours," Zara replied. "Maybe less."

"Right then," he said, moving toward the helm despite her medical advice about rest and recovery. "Time to move."

"You're injured and medicated," she protested. "You need to stay in bed and let the antibiotics work."

"I need to keep my crew alive," he replied firmly. "Bed rest can wait until we're not being hunted by military assassins."

The next hour was controlled chaos as they prepared for emergency departure. Viktor watched their preparations with obvious interest, his dead eyes calculating angles and opportunities while they secured equipment and plotted escape routes.

"Where we heading?" Miguel asked, studying charts while Jin monitored communications for signs of approaching threats.

"Deep water," Ryder decided, his tactical thinking clear despite the fever and medication. "If they want to use military vessels against us, we'll make them work for it in open ocean."

"In your condition?" Tomás asked with concern. "Deep water operations require full crew capability."

"I'll manage," Ryder said, though Zara could see the effort it cost him to maintain focus.

"No, you won't," she said firmly, making a decision that surprised even herself. "I'll take the helm. You navigate and coordinate, but I'm driving."

The look he gave her was equal parts surprise and admiration.

"You sure about that, love?" he asked. "These aren't Miami recreational waters."

"I'm sure," she replied, moving to the helm with confidence she hoped she actually possessed. "Uncle Ronny taught me to handle boats in conditions that would make Coast Guard instructors cry."

"Fair dinkum," Ryder said with a slight grin. "Let's see what you can do."

The *Siren's Call* departed their hidden anchorage just as the first military helicopter appeared on the horizon. The timing was close enough to suggest satellite surveillance had tracked their movements exactly as Martinez had claimed.

"Contact bearing north-northeast," Jin reported from the radar station. "Multiple aircraft, probably helicopter gunships."

"And surface vessels approaching from the south," Tomás added, monitoring marine radar frequencies. "Fast attack craft, military configuration."

"They're boxing us in," Zara observed, studying the tactical situation while pushing the boat to maximum speed. "Classic military interdiction pattern."

"Then we don't go where they expect," Ryder said, his navigation skills unimpaired despite his medical condition. "Deep water trench system, forty miles east. Complex underwater terrain that'll complicate their sonar tracking."

The run toward deep water was harrowing, with military aircraft and vessels converging from multiple directions while Zara pushed the *Siren's Call* to her limits. The boat handled beautifully under her guidance, responding to steering inputs with the kind of precision that came from expert design and maintenance.

"You're a bloody natural," Ryder said with admiration as she threaded their course between coral reefs and shallow patches that could ground pursuing vessels.

"Told you Uncle Ronny knew what he was doing," she replied, concentration absolute as she navigated by chart and instinct through water that was becoming increasingly challenging.

The military pursuit force was professional and determined, but they were also operating under rules of engagement that limited their options. Destroying a civilian vessel in international waters, even with authorization, required careful documentation and strategic justification.

That hesitation gave the *Siren's Call* the edge she needed to reach the deep water trench system, where underwater terrain and thermal layers would complicate sonar tracking and make coordinated assault more difficult.

"Lost them," Jin reported with satisfaction as they entered water over two thousand feet deep. "Radar contacts fading, probably due to thermal interference from the trench system."

"How long before they relocate us?" Miguel asked.

"Depends on their resources and patience," Ryder replied, studying charts of the trench system with tactical interest.

"But we've bought ourselves some time to figure out next moves."

The immediate crisis had passed, but their long-term situation remained desperate. Viktor's criminal network had military-grade resources and government protection, while they had one treasure hunting vessel and evidence that couldn't be delivered to authorities without exposing themselves to assassination.

"We need legitimate federal contact," Zara said, voicing what they were all thinking. "Someone in law enforcement who's not corrupt."

"Any ideas who that might be?" Ryder asked.

"Maybe," she replied, thinking of federal agents she'd worked with who had reputations for integrity. "But contacting them means risking exposure to Martinez's network."

"Risk we'll have to take," he said simply. "Can't fight international criminal organizations without some kind of official support."

The afternoon wore on with cautious navigation through the trench system while they debated options and monitored communications for signs of continued pursuit. Viktor remained silent but watchful, clearly waiting for opportunities to exploit their situation.

As evening approached, Ryder's condition began deteriorating again despite the antibiotic treatment. His fever was climbing, and the infection was showing signs of spreading beyond the original wound site.

"You need to rest," Zara said, helping him to the small medical station in the boat's main cabin. "The antibiotics are working, but your body needs time to fight the infection."

"Can't afford to rest," he protested, though his movements were becoming increasingly unsteady. "Crew needs leadership, mission needs coordination."

"Crew needs you alive more than they need you conscious," she pointed out, helping him lie down on the narrow medical bunk. "Miguel and Jin can handle boat operations. Let your body heal."

The medical station was cramped, barely large enough for the bunk and basic equipment, but it provided privacy and quiet that the main cabin couldn't offer. Zara checked his temperature and wound dressing, satisfied that the infection wasn't spreading but concerned about his overall condition.

"You saved my life," he said quietly, his fever-bright eyes studying her face in the dim light from the overhead lamp.

"You saved mine first," she replied, adjusting his blankets and checking the IV line she'd established to maintain his antibiotic levels. "Guess we're even."

"Not even close to even," he disagreed, his hand finding hers and holding it with surprising strength. "You could have disappeared with that evidence, gone back to your federal life, left us to deal with Viktor's people alone."

"I told you before," she said, squeezing his hand gently. "I'd rather have you as a partner than as someone I betrayed."

"Partner," he repeated, testing the word again. "Professional and personal?"

"Everything," she confirmed, leaning closer to check his pulse and finding herself caught by the intensity in his green eyes.

"I'm falling in love with you," he said simply, the words carrying weight despite his weakened condition. "Probably have been since you told me the truth about being a federal agent."

The admission hit her harder than expected, cutting through professional protocols and emotional defenses she'd maintained for years. Federal agents weren't supposed to fall in love during operations, weren't supposed to let personal feelings compromise mission objectives.

But looking at this man who'd risked everything to help her mission, who'd been wounded defending evidence that could clear his brother's name, she couldn't deny her own feelings any longer.

"I'm falling in love with you too," she admitted, her voice barely above a whisper. "Scared the hell out of me, but it's true."

The space between them seemed to shrink as he pulled her closer, mindful of his shoulder injury but needing the physical connection that confirmed their emotional bond.

"This is crazy," she said, even as she settled beside him on the narrow bunk. "We're being hunted by international criminals and corrupt federal agents, and I'm falling for a treasure hunter who makes me forget about everything except how he makes me feel."

"How do I make you feel?" he asked, his voice rough with emotion and fever.

"Safe," she said honestly. "Protected. Like someone finally understands who I really am instead of just seeing the federal agent or the cover identity."

"You make me feel alive again," he replied, his fingers tracing the line of her jaw with gentle pressure. "Like there's something worth fighting for besides just clearing Marcus's name."

The kiss was soft and careful, mindful of his medical condition but full of emotion that had been building between them for days. Salt air and antiseptic couldn't mask the essential taste of him, the way his lips moved against hers with increasing hunger despite his weakness.

"You sure about this?" she asked, aware of his injury and the cramped conditions of the medical station. "You need rest, not..."

"Need you more than rest," he said firmly, his hands working at the buttons of her shirt with careful determination. "Need to feel you close to me, need to know this is real."

The medical station's narrow bunk barely accommodated one person, let alone two, but they made it work through careful positioning and attention to his injured shoulder. When her

"I love you," he said again as he filled her with his cum, the words mixing with groans of pleasure and satisfaction.

They stayed connected afterward, breathing hard in the cramped space while their heartbeats gradually returned to normal. The medical station felt like their own private world, isolated from the dangers outside and the uncertain future they faced.

"What happens now?" she asked eventually, her head resting on his uninjured shoulder.

"Now we clear Marcus's name, expose Martinez and Viktor's network, and figure out how to have a relationship when this is all over," he replied with the kind of confidence that made her believe anything was possible.

"That's a lot of complications," she pointed out.

"Best things in life usually are," he said, pressing a soft kiss to her forehead. "Worth it though, if we can pull it off."

Outside their intimate sanctuary, the Caribbean night stretched endlessly, hiding secrets and dangers that would test everything they'd built together. But for now, they had each other, and that felt like enough to face whatever came next.

The ocean kept its secrets, but some truths were worth diving deep to find.

CHAPTER SEVEN

Dawn broke over the Caribbean deep water like spilled gold, painting the endless blue in shades that would have been beautiful under different circumstances. But Zara couldn't appreciate the sunrise while watching radar contacts multiply on Jin's electronics display, showing the coordinated approach of what looked like a full military operation.

"Eight vessels, multiple aircraft, classic federal interdiction formation," Jin reported from her station, her Korean accent adding precision to the technical briefing. "Someone called in serious backup."

"Martinez," Zara said with certainty, studying the electronic signatures while Ryder recovered in the medical station. His fever had broken during the night, and the antibiotics were finally winning the battle against infection, but he was still weak from the ordeal.

Viktor sat in the main cabin, zip-tied to a chair but watching everything with those dead eyes that missed nothing. The Russian arms dealer had been silent since his capture, but Zara could practically see him calculating odds and angles, waiting for his opportunity.

"Federal backup or federal execution squad?" Miguel asked, checking his sidearm while studying the approaching fleet through binoculars.

"With Martinez coordinating, probably both," Zara replied grimly. "She'll have legitimate Coast Guard units mixed with corrupt military contractors. Gives her deniability when witnesses disappear."

The *Siren's Call* drifted in water over three thousand feet deep, hidden among the thermal layers that complicated sonar detection. But their concealment wouldn't last long against a coordinated search operation with the resources Martinez was deploying.

"We got maybe thirty minutes before they get close enough for visual identification," Tomás estimated, studying the radar contacts' approach vectors. "After that, we're fucked."

"Not necessarily," Zara said, an idea forming as she watched the tactical display. "Martinez is coordinating this through federal channels, which means she has to follow some kind of protocol. She can't just have eight boats open fire on a civilian vessel without documentation."

"So?" Miguel asked.

"So she needs a reason to justify lethal force," Zara explained, her federal training providing insight into bureaucratic requirements. "She'll stage an incident, make it look like we fired first or posed an immediate threat."

"False flag operation," Ryder said, appearing in the doorway despite her medical orders to stay in bed. His color was better and the fever-brightness had left his green eyes, but he still moved carefully to avoid stressing his injured shoulder.

"Exactly," Zara confirmed. "She'll have legitimate Coast Guard units respond to a fake distress call or terrorist threat, while her corrupt people position for the actual assault."

"Which means some of those boats are really trying to help us," Jin observed, studying the electronic signatures more carefully. "And some are trying to kill us."

"Problem is figuring out which is which," Miguel added.

The tactical situation was complex and dangerous - multiple federal agencies responding to conflicting information while corrupt elements tried to eliminate witnesses. One wrong move could trigger a firefight between legitimate law enforcement and criminal conspirators.

"There," Zara said, pointing to two contacts approaching from the southeast. "Those are Coast Guard cutters, proper federal vessels responding to Martinez's false intelligence. The others..."

"Military contractors posing as federal backup," Ryder finished, his naval experience reading the tactical display with professional interest. "Classic misdirection - use legitimate authority to mask criminal operations."

The radio crackled with official-sounding communications as the approaching vessels coordinated their search pattern. But Zara's trained ear caught subtle differences between genuine federal communications and the too-precise military jargon of professional contractors.

"Coast Guard Cutter *Resolute* to all vessels," came an authoritative voice over the emergency frequency. "We are responding to reports of terrorist activity and stolen federal evidence. All civilian vessels clear the area immediately."

"Terrorist activity," Miguel repeated with dark humor. "Guess we got promoted from treasure hunters."

"Martinez is covering all the bases," Zara said. "Terrorism charges justify lethal force and military intervention. Plus it explains why federal evidence recovery requires special operations."

"Right then," Ryder decided, moving to the helm despite Zara's protests about his medical condition. "Time to call Martinez's bluff."

"What you thinking?" she asked, recognizing the calculating look that meant he was planning something dangerous.

"We contact the real Coast Guard directly," he said, reaching for the radio. "Emergency frequency, full federal identification, request immediate assistance."

"That'll expose our position to everyone," Jin pointed out.

"Already exposed," Ryder replied. "But it'll also force Martinez to show her hand. She can't have legitimate Coast Guard units witness whatever her contractors are planning."

The radio call went out on Coast Guard emergency frequency, Zara's federal credentials providing authentication while they requested immediate assistance from legitimate law enforcement. The response was swift and professional, exactly what she'd expect from real federal backup.

"Agent Baptiste, this is Coast Guard Cutter *Resolute*," came the crisp reply. "We show your position in deep water approximately forty miles southeast of Nassau. What is the nature of your emergency?"

"Federal agent under assault by corrupt military contractors," Zara replied, giving the Coast Guard captain enough information to understand the gravity without revealing operational details. "Request immediate assistance and federal backup."

The silence that followed was telling. Real Coast Guard captains didn't hesitate when federal agents requested emergency assistance.

"Agent Baptiste," the voice returned, but something had changed in the tone. "We need you to maintain your current position while we coordinate with other federal agencies in the area."

Translation: Martinez was monitoring Coast Guard communications and coordinating her response to eliminate witnesses before legitimate backup could intervene.

"They're stalling," Ryder observed, studying the tactical display as the approaching vessels adjusted their formation. "Legitimate Coast Guard would be racing to assist a federal agent under attack."

"Martinez got to them," Zara realized with growing alarm. "Either directly or through false intelligence that makes us look like the criminals."

The next few minutes were crucial as various federal agencies tried to sort out conflicting information while Martinez's people positioned for their assault. Multiple radio frequencies buzzed with official-sounding coordination that masked the criminal conspiracy underneath.

"Contact bearing north-northwest," Jin announced, studying new radar signatures. "Fast attack boats, military configuration, closing rapidly."

"Those aren't Coast Guard," Miguel identified, watching through binoculars as sleek military vessels approached at high speed. "Professional hardware, probably special operations."

"Martinez's kill squad," Zara said with certainty. "Here to eliminate all witnesses and recover the evidence."

Viktor chose that moment to speak for the first time since his capture, his Russian-accented voice carrying dark amusement.

"Agent Martinez has been very thorough," he said with satisfaction. "Military contractors, corrupt Coast Guard officers, federal agencies feeding each other false intelligence. You cannot trust anyone."

"We'll see about that," Zara replied, but part of her wondered if the Russian was right. How deep did the corruption go? How many federal agencies had been compromised by diamond trafficking money?

"Incoming," Tomás called from the weather station, pointing toward military helicopters approaching from multiple directions. "Air support, heavy weapons, coordinated assault formation."

The *Siren's Call* was surrounded by overwhelming force - Coast Guard cutters that might or might not be legitimate, military contractors with authorization to eliminate threats, and helicopter gunships that could destroy their boat with a single missile.

"Time to go," Ryder decided, pushing the engines to maximum power despite their desperate tactical situation.

"Go where?" Miguel asked. "They got us surrounded."

"Not surrounded," Ryder corrected with the kind of grin that had probably gotten him in trouble during his naval service. "Contained. Different tactical situation entirely."

The distinction became clear as Ryder began maneuvering through the approaching vessels with precision that spoke to years of military experience. Instead of trying to outrun superior forces, he was using their coordination against them, forcing multiple agencies to avoid collision while creating confusion about his intentions.

"He's playing them against each other," Jin observed with admiration as Coast Guard vessels found themselves dangerously close to military contractors that weren't supposed to be operating in federal waters.

"Exactly," Zara said, understanding Ryder's tactical thinking. "Force Martinez to choose between maintaining her cover story and eliminating witnesses."

The choice came when one of the military contractors, frustrated by the *Siren's Call's* evasive maneuvers, opened fire with automatic weapons despite the presence of legitimate Coast Guard vessels.

"Shots fired, shots fired," came the immediate response from Coast Guard Cutter *Resolute*. "Unknown vessel is firing on civilian craft, all units respond."

The radio erupted with confused communications as legitimate federal personnel tried to understand why military contractors were shooting at a boat that was supposed to contain federal agents requesting assistance.

"Now we got them," Zara said with satisfaction. "Martinez can't explain why her people are shooting at federal agents without blowing her cover."

But the tactical situation remained desperate. Caught between legitimate Coast Guard units that didn't understand the full situation and military contractors with orders to eliminate all witnesses, the *Siren's Call* was running out of maneuvering room.

"There," Ryder pointed toward a gap between two Coast Guard vessels where confusion about the engagement rules had created a brief opening. "Window of opportunity."

The next few minutes were some of the most harrowing in Zara's federal career as Ryder threaded their boat through a complex maritime battle involving multiple agencies firing on each other while trying to sort out who were the good guys.

Military contractors engaged Coast Guard cutters that were trying to protect what they thought was a federal agent under attack. Helicopter gunships found themselves unable to fire without risking legitimate federal personnel. And through the chaos, the *Siren's Call* raced toward open water while radio frequencies buzzed with increasingly desperate attempts at coordination.

"Coast Guard Cutter *Resolute* to all vessels," came an authoritative voice that cut through the communications chaos. "Cease fire, cease fire. We have federal agents aboard the civilian vessel requesting protection from hostile forces."

"Hostile forces, stand down immediately," another voice added with command authority that suggested senior federal leadership. "You are firing on legitimate law enforcement personnel."

"Who the hell is that?" Miguel asked, studying the radio display while Zara worked to identify the new voice cutting through Martinez's carefully orchestrated confusion.

"Real federal backup," she said with hope and relief. "Someone Martinez doesn't control."

The new voice belonged to Deputy Director James Harrison, DEA Operations, a man with thirty years of federal law enforcement experience and a reputation for absolute integrity. If Harrison was involved, it meant someone at the highest levels had realized the scope of Martinez's corruption.

"Agent Sarah Martinez, you are ordered to stand down all operations and report for immediate debriefing," Harrison's voice commanded over official federal frequency. "Any interference with this operation will be considered obstruction of federal justice."

The silence that followed was profound. Martinez's carefully coordinated assault had just been countermanded by someone with authority to destroy her career and send her to federal prison.

"Agent Baptiste," Harrison's voice continued, addressing her directly. "This is Deputy Director Harrison, DEA Operations. We are aware of your situation and have legitimate federal backup en route. Maintain your position and avoid engagement with any vessels not specifically identified as authorized federal law enforcement."

"Copy that, Deputy Director," Zara replied, relief flooding through her voice. "We have recovered significant evidence of international diamond trafficking and federal corruption. Also holding one high-value prisoner."

"Understood," Harrison replied. "Federal evidence recovery team will coordinate with Coast Guard for secure transfer. Be advised, we have multiple agencies responding with conflicting intelligence, so maintain defensive posture until situation is clarified."

The tactical display began showing new contacts approaching from the northeast - legitimate federal vessels with proper identification and authorization codes that even Martinez couldn't counterfeit.

"Cavalry's coming," Ryder observed with satisfaction, studying the approaching federal backup. "Question is whether Martinez's people will try one last play before legitimate authority takes control."

The answer came in the form of Viktor's low chuckle from his chair in the main cabin.

"Agent Martinez is more resourceful than you imagine," he said with dark amusement. "She will not allow herself to be captured when so much money is at stake."

"What's that supposed to mean?" Zara demanded, moving closer to their prisoner.

"It means you have been thinking like federal agents instead of criminals," Viktor replied. "Martinez does not intend to be arrested. She intends to disappear with enough evidence and money to start over somewhere beyond federal reach."

The implication hit Zara like a physical blow. Martinez wasn't planning to fight legitimate federal backup - she was planning to eliminate all evidence of her corruption and escape while the various agencies sorted out the chaos she'd created.

"The diamonds," she realized with growing alarm. "She knows where we hid them in the *Caribbean Star* wreck."

"And she has the resources to recover them while federal agencies are busy investigating each other," Viktor added with malicious satisfaction.

"Bloody hell," Ryder said, understanding immediately. "While we're dealing with legitimate Coast Guard debriefing and evidence transfer, Martinez's people are looting the wreck site."

The radio crackled with new communications as Deputy Director Harrison coordinated federal response, but his legitimate backup was still twenty minutes away. More than enough time for Martinez to recover the hidden diamonds and eliminate the primary evidence against her criminal network.

"We have to go back," Zara said, making a decision that went against every federal protocol she'd been trained to follow. "Can't let her steal that evidence."

"Go back where?" Miguel asked. "The wreck site? That's exactly where Martinez expects us to go."

"Doesn't matter what she expects," Zara replied firmly. "Those diamonds are evidence of war crimes and federal corruption. Without them, Viktor's testimony won't be enough to bring down the entire network."

"She's right," Ryder agreed, already changing course toward the *Caribbean Star* coordinates despite the danger. "We didn't come this far to let corruption win because we followed proper procedures."

The decision to return to the wreck site was tactically insane and professionally indefensible. But it was also the only way to ensure that months of investigation and personal sacrifice would result in actual justice rather than bureaucratic cover-ups.

"Deputy Director Harrison," Zara called on federal frequency, "be advised we are returning to original evidence location to prevent tampering by corrupt personnel."

"Agent Baptiste," Harrison's voice carried sharp concern, "you are ordered to maintain position and await federal backup. Do not engage hostile forces without proper support."

"Copy your orders, sir," she replied. "But respectfully, evidence preservation takes priority over agent safety."

"Agent Baptiste..." Harrison began, but Zara switched to a different frequency, cutting off official protests that would only waste time.

"He's gonna be pissed," Miguel observed.

"Better pissed than letting war criminals escape with fifty million in blood diamonds," she replied, her Miami street attitude overriding federal bureaucracy.

The run back to the *Caribbean Star* coordinates took forty minutes of high-speed navigation through increasingly rough seas. Weather was building again from the northwest, and the combination of wind and waves made boat handling challenging even for Ryder's expert seamanship.

"Contact on site," Jin reported as they approached the wreck coordinates. "Large vessel, dive operations active, multiple small boats providing security."

"Martinez's recovery operation," Tomás identified, studying the vessels through binoculars. "Professional setup, serious equipment, they're not playing around."

The scene at the wreck site was exactly what Viktor had predicted - a coordinated diamond recovery operation disguised as federal evidence collection. Martinez's people were systematically looting the hidden caches while maintaining the appearance of legitimate law enforcement activity.

"How many?" Ryder asked, studying the tactical situation with naval interest.

"Main recovery vessel plus four security boats," Jin replied, monitoring radio communications. "Professional crew, military equipment, probably twenty personnel total."

"And us," Miguel added, checking his weapons. "Five people, one boat, limited firepower."

"Six people," Viktor corrected from his chair, still secured by zip-ties. "I am still here, and I have no interest in letting Martinez steal diamonds that belong to my organization."

"You're tied up and under arrest," Zara pointed out.

"Which does not change the fact that Martinez has been systematically stealing from my operations," Viktor replied with that dead-eyed smile. "My associates were already en route to address her theft before your federal raid complicated matters."

The suggestion was intriguing but didn't require federal cooperation with a war criminal. If Viktor's people were already hunting Martinez for stealing from their operations, that could work in their favor without compromising federal protocols.

"Your people are already coming?" Zara asked, studying the tactical situation while keeping Viktor securely restrained.

"Martinez's theft from my organization predates her conflict with federal agencies," Viktor confirmed, remaining cuffed to his chair. "Two patrol boats, heavily armed, very motivated to recover stolen property. They do not distinguish between federal thieves and criminal thieves."

"When?" Ryder asked with tactical interest.

"Soon," Viktor said with satisfaction. "My associates do not appreciate theft, regardless of the source."

The tactical mathematics were still challenging. Martinez's forces outnumbered them four to one and had superior equipment. But if Viktor's people were already hunting the same target for their own reasons...

"We don't work with you," Zara said firmly to Viktor. "But if your people want to settle their own scores with Martinez, that's between criminal organizations."

"Pragmatic," Viktor agreed, still secured to his chair. "My associates will pursue their own interests. What you do with the resulting chaos is your federal prerogative."

The approach of Viktor's patrol boats was announced by Jin's radar monitoring rather than any communication from their prisoner.

"Contact," she reported, studying electronic signatures. "Two vessels approaching from the northeast, military configuration, high speed."

"Viktor's people," Miguel identified, watching through binoculars as sleek patrol boats appeared on the horizon.

"They don't waste time," Ryder observed with naval appreciation, studying the approaching vessels that moved with professional precision.

"Profit and survival," Viktor said from his restraints with obvious satisfaction. "Powerful motivations for rapid response."

The patrol boats approached the battle scene with the kind of aggressive maneuvering that suggested serious combat capability. They ignored the *Siren's Call* entirely, focusing on Martinez's forces with the single-minded purpose of criminal organizations settling disputes through violence.

"They're not here for rescue," Zara observed, watching Viktor's boats position for assault on Martinez's diamond recovery operation.

"They're here for revenge," Viktor confirmed with dark amusement. "Martinez cost my organization considerable profits. My associates intend to recover their losses with interest."

The next hour was controlled chaos as Viktor's patrol boats engaged Martinez's security forces while the *Siren's Call* made her approach to the main recovery vessel. The battle was intense but brief - Viktor's people had superior firepower and the advantage of surprise.

Martinez's radio voice cut through the combat communications with frustrated anger.

"All units, priority target is the civilian vessel carrying federal evidence," she commanded. "Eliminate all witnesses and secure the recovered materials."

"Negative," came an unexpected response from one of her own boats. "We have Coast Guard identification on approach, federal backup is two minutes out."

Deputy Director Harrison's legitimate federal backup had finally arrived, approaching the battle scene with proper authority and overwhelming force. Martinez's carefully planned evidence theft was collapsing under the weight of real law enforcement response.

"Time to go," Viktor said with casual indifference as his patrol boats completed their assault on Martinez's forces. "My business here is finished."

"Not quite," Zara said, showing him the federal handcuffs she'd palmed while cutting his restraints. "You're still under arrest for international arms dealing and war crimes."

Viktor's dead eyes showed genuine surprise for the first time since his capture.

"You would arrest me after I helped you recover your evidence?" he asked.

"I'd arrest you because you're a war criminal who profits from human misery," she replied firmly. "Temporary cooperation doesn't change that."

The handcuffs clicked into place with satisfying finality as legitimate Coast Guard vessels surrounded the wreck site, establishing federal authority over what had become an international incident involving multiple criminal organizations.

"Agent Baptiste," Deputy Director Harrison's voice came over the radio with relief and exasperation. "Report your status and prepare for evidence transfer."

"All secure, sir," she replied, watching Martinez's remaining forces surrender to overwhelming federal backup. "Evidence recovered, primary suspect in custody, corrupt handler's operations disrupted."

"And Agent Martinez?" Harrison asked.

Zara looked toward the main recovery vessel where federal agents were taking corrupt personnel into custody. Among the prisoners being led away in handcuffs, she spotted Martinez's familiar figure.

"In federal custody," she confirmed with satisfaction. "Along with enough evidence to dismantle her entire criminal network."

The Caribbean sun was setting as federal evidence teams catalogued the recovered diamonds and documented the scope of the international trafficking operation. Months of investigation and personal risk had finally resulted in justice for the victims of conflict diamond trafficking.

"Think it's over?" Ryder asked, standing beside her as they watched federal agents coordinate the massive evidence recovery.

"This part is," she replied, leaning against his uninjured shoulder while watching the sunset paint the ocean in shades of gold and crimson. "Martinez is finished, Viktor's in custody, and the diamonds are back in federal hands."

"What about us?" he asked quietly. "What happens when the federal debriefing is finished and you go back to your regular life?"

She looked at this man who'd risked everything to help her mission, who'd been wounded defending evidence that could clear his brother's name, who'd made her feel things she'd never experienced in years of federal service.

"Maybe my regular life needs some changes," she said, surprising herself with the certainty in her voice. "Maybe it's time to find out what comes after justice."

The ocean stretched endlessly around them, keeping its secrets while new ones were being written. They had evidence, they had justice, and they had each other.

Time to find out what that combination was worth.

CHAPTER EIGHT

Viktor Kozlov sat in federal custody aboard Coast Guard Cutter *Resolute*, handcuffed and under armed guard, but his dead eyes held the kind of satisfaction that made Zara's skin crawl. For a man facing life in federal prison for war crimes and international arms dealing, he looked remarkably pleased with himself.

"Something you find funny about federal charges?" she asked, studying his expression while Deputy Director Harrison coordinated the massive evidence recovery operation around the *Caribbean Star* wreck site.

"I find it amusing that you believe capturing me ends anything," Viktor replied in his Russian-accented English. "I am one man in a very large organization, Agent Baptiste. My associates do not appreciate interference with their operations."

The words carried weight that made Zara's federal training alert her to immediate threat. International criminal organizations didn't just disappear when their leaders were arrested - they retaliated against the people who'd caused them problems.

"What kind of retaliation?" she asked, though she suspected she already knew the answer.

"The kind that makes federal agents very cooperative," Viktor said with that dead-eyed smile. "Your family in Miami, for instance. Very exposed, very vulnerable."

Zara's blood went cold. Her parents still lived in the Little Haiti house where she'd grown up, and her younger brother Carlos worked construction around Miami-Dade. None of them had federal protection because her undercover operation was supposed to be completely secret.

"If anything happens to my family," she said quietly, her voice carrying the kind of flat calm that meant serious violence was being considered.

"Nothing will happen to them if you cooperate," Viktor interrupted. "My associates simply require certain assurances about the evidence you've recovered."

"You want me to tamper with federal evidence."

"I want you to ensure that certain documents and recordings do not reach federal prosecutors," Viktor clarified. "Small omissions that would protect ongoing operations without compromising your precious case against me."

The proposal was elegant in its corruption - Viktor would accept conviction on lesser charges if his criminal network could continue operating without interference from the evidence Zara had recovered.

"No deal," she said firmly. "That evidence goes to federal prosecutors exactly as recovered."

"Then your family becomes a priority target for my associates," Viktor replied with casual indifference. "They are very skilled at making examples that other federal agents remember."

Deputy Director Harrison appeared beside them, his weathered face showing the strain of coordinating multiple federal agencies in the aftermath of Martinez's corruption.

"Agent Baptiste," he said, "we need to discuss debriefing procedures and witness protection protocols."

"Sir, we might have a problem," she said, explaining Viktor's threats against her family while the Russian listened with obvious amusement.

Harrison's expression darkened as he processed the implications.

"How specific was the threat?" he asked.

"Specific enough," Viktor answered before Zara could respond. "My associates have been monitoring federal personnel involved in diamond trafficking investigations. Agent Baptiste's family members are well-documented targets."

"We'll arrange immediate protection," Harrison decided. "Federal marshals, safe house procedures, full witness protection protocols."

"That won't be sufficient," Viktor said with confidence. "My organization has resources that exceed federal protective capabilities. Better to negotiate reasonable cooperation than watch innocent people suffer for Agent Baptiste's stubbornness."

The casual way he discussed murdering her family made Zara want to throw him overboard and watch him drown. But her federal training kept her focused on protecting the people she loved rather than satisfying her desire for revenge.

"How long to get federal protection in place?" she asked Harrison.

"Six hours minimum," he replied with professional honesty. "Coordinating with Miami field office, arranging safe houses, establishing security protocols - these things take time."

"Time my family might not have," Zara said, her Miami accent thickening with stress as she processed the tactical situation.

"There is another option," Viktor said, clearly enjoying the leverage his threats provided. "My associates are operating from a secure facility approximately thirty miles southwest of here. Underwater cave complex, natural formation enhanced with military-grade security."

"Why would you tell us that?" Ryder asked, joining the conversation after securing his boat's integration with the federal evidence recovery operation.

"Because I am offering a trade," Viktor replied. "Agent Baptiste recovers certain specific items from my associates' facility, and her family remains safe. Everyone wins."

"What kind of items?" Harrison asked, his federal experience recognizing the smell of a setup.

"Communication equipment, operational records, certain financial documents," Viktor said vaguely. "Nothing that would compromise your case against me, but items that would be... inconvenient... if they reached federal prosecutors."

The offer was obviously a trap, but it was also potentially their only chance to neutralize the threat against Zara's family before Viktor's associates could act on their retaliation plans.

"It's a setup," Ryder said bluntly. "He wants to lure us into his people's stronghold where they can eliminate all witnesses."

"Of course it's a setup," Viktor agreed with amusement. "But it's also your only realistic option for protecting Agent Baptiste's family before my associates demonstrate their commitment to organizational security."

Harrison studied the tactical situation with thirty years of federal law enforcement experience, weighing risks against potential outcomes.

"We could coordinate federal assault on the facility," he suggested. "Military support, proper backup, overwhelming force."

"Coordinate with whom?" Viktor asked pointedly. "Agent Martinez corrupted federal communications for three years. How many other agents in your organization have been compromised? How many of your 'federal assault teams' would report your plans directly to my associates?"

The question hit harder than expected because it was probably accurate. Martinez's corruption had revealed how deeply criminal organizations had penetrated federal law enforcement. Any large-scale operation would risk exposure to remaining moles.

"Small team," Zara decided, her federal training adapting to circumstances that weren't covered in academy protocols. "Minimal federal exposure, limited communications, surgical approach. When agent safety and family protection conflict with standard procedure, emergency protocols give field agents discretionary authority."

"That's suicide," Harrison protested. "Viktor's facility is probably defended by professional military contractors with superior firepower."

"Maybe," she agreed. "But it's also our only chance to neutralize the threat before my family gets hurt."

"I'm going with her," Ryder said simply, his Australian accent carrying the kind of finality that suggested the decision wasn't negotiable.

"This is a federal operation," Harrison pointed out. "Civilian involvement is against regulations."

"Fuck regulations," Zara said bluntly, her Miami street attitude overriding federal protocols. "My family is in danger because I did my job too well. I'm going after Viktor's people with whatever help I can get."

The next two hours were spent in intensive planning as they prepared for an assault on Viktor's underwater cave facility. Federal resources were limited due to security concerns, but Harrison provided what support he could without risking exposure to remaining criminal moles.

Miguel and Jin volunteered for the mission despite the obvious dangers, their loyalty to Ryder and respect for Zara making them willing to risk their lives for her family's safety. Tomás remained with the *Siren's Call* to coordinate communications and emergency extraction if the mission went wrong.

"Cave diving is extremely dangerous," Miguel warned as they prepared technical diving equipment for the underwater approach. "Different from open water diving - no direct access to surface, limited air supply, easy to get lost or trapped."

"I grew up diving Caribbean caves," Zara said, her cultural background providing advantages that federal training couldn't replicate. "Uncle Ronny taught me and my cousins every cave system from Key Largo to Biscayne Bay."

"This won't be recreational cave diving," Ryder pointed out, checking his rebreather system and underwater weapons. "Viktor's people will have military-grade defenses and professional security."

"Then we better be professional too," she replied, testing her own equipment with the kind of careful attention that meant the difference between success and death in underwater operations.

Viktor watched their preparations with obvious interest, his handcuffs securing him to a chair in the Coast Guard cutter's main cabin while federal agents coordinated the mission around him.

"You will find my associates more resourceful than you expect," he said to Zara as she completed her equipment check. "They have been operating in Caribbean waters for many years."

"We'll see about that," she replied, refusing to let him see any doubt or fear that might encourage his criminal network.

The approach to Viktor's cave facility required two hours of careful navigation through reef systems and shallow water that would challenge pursuit vessels. The entrance was hidden among natural coral formations, nearly invisible from the surface but identifiable to divers who knew what to look for.

"There," Zara pointed to a dark opening in the reef wall, barely large enough for a person to swim through. "Cave entrance, maybe forty feet down, natural formation."

"Tight squeeze," Miguel observed, studying the opening through his diving mask. "Once we're inside, retreat becomes very difficult."

"That's why it's a good defensive position," Ryder said, his naval training analyzing the tactical advantages of the underwater fortress. "Control the entrance, control access."

The cave system beyond the entrance was larger than expected, with multiple chambers connected by underwater passages that had been enhanced with artificial lighting and breathing stations. Viktor's people had turned a natural cave network into a sophisticated underwater facility.

"Motion sensors," Jin warned, studying her electronics while they swam through the submerged tunnels. "They know we're here."

"Expected," Zara replied, her federal training prepared for detection during tactical infiltration. "Question is how they respond."

The answer came in the form of underwater guards armed with spear guns and military diving equipment. Professional security that moved through the cave system with familiarity that suggested years of operation.

The underwater combat that followed was unlike anything in Zara's federal experience. Fighting for your life in confined spaces with limited air supply while armed men tried to spear you like fish required skills that combined federal training with Caribbean cultural knowledge.

"Cave current," she warned Ryder as they maneuvered through a particularly narrow passage. "Water flow will affect spear gun accuracy."

"Fair dinkum," he replied, using the current to avoid a spear that would have punched through his diving equipment. "These bastards know their business."

The facility's main chamber was an air-filled cave large enough to accommodate boats and equipment storage. Professional setup with communication gear, weapons racks, and what looked like operational headquarters for ongoing criminal activities.

"Documents," Jin identified, pointing toward filing cabinets and computer equipment that represented the kind of evidence that could expose Viktor's entire criminal network.

"And hostages," Miguel added grimly, indicating three people zip-tied to chairs near the communication station.

Zara's heart nearly stopped when she recognized two of the hostages. Her younger brother Carlos and her cousin Marie, both unconscious but alive, being held as leverage against her cooperation.

"They got my family," she said, federal protocols and tactical planning disappearing in the face of personal threat.

"Easy," Ryder warned, his hand on her arm as she started toward the hostages. "This is exactly what Viktor's people want - emotional reaction that compromises tactical thinking."

He was right, but seeing her family in danger made it almost impossible to maintain professional detachment. These were people she'd grown up with, shared family holidays and cultural traditions, protected since childhood.

"Agent Baptiste," a voice called from the shadows near the equipment racks. "Welcome to our facility."

The man who emerged was tall and pale, with the kind of military bearing that suggested special forces background.

Professional killer, almost certainly, and someone with enough authority to negotiate on behalf of Viktor's organization.

"I am Colonel Petrov," he continued in Russian-accented English. "Viktor's operational commander for Caribbean activities."

"Let my family go," Zara demanded, her federal training struggling with personal emotions. "They're civilians, not part of this operation."

"They became part of it when you interfered with our business," Petrov replied with cold professionalism. "Now they provide motivation for your cooperation."

"What kind of cooperation?"

"Simple trade," Petrov said, gesturing toward the computer equipment and files. "You destroy certain operational records, eliminate specific evidence from your federal case, and your family members are released unharmed."

The same offer Viktor had made, but with immediate family members as hostages to ensure compliance. Elegant in its simplicity and brutal in its effectiveness.

"And if I refuse?"

"Then your brother and cousin become examples of what happens to people who interfere with our organization," Petrov said with casual indifference. "Very public examples that other federal agents will remember."

Zara looked at Carlos and Marie, unconscious but alive, then at the evidence that could expose years of criminal activity and prevent future atrocities. Federal agent versus family member, professional duty versus personal loyalty, justice versus love.

"I need to see the evidence first," she said, buying time while Ryder and the crew positioned themselves for whatever action became necessary.

"Of course," Petrov agreed, leading her toward the computer station while his armed guards maintained overwatch. "You will find it very comprehensive."

The files were exactly what Viktor had described - operational records, financial accounts, communication logs, and documentation of criminal activities spanning multiple countries and organizations. Destroying this evidence would cripple federal prosecution of the entire network.

But it would also save her family's lives.

"Impressive operation," she admitted, studying the scope of Viktor's criminal empire while calculating tactical options.

"Very profitable," Petrov agreed. "Worth protecting from federal interference."

"I can see that," Zara said, her hand moving toward the computer keyboard while her federal training fought with family loyalty.

Then she heard it - a soft sound that made her heart race with hope. Uncle Ronny's whistle, the two-tone call he'd taught all his nieces and nephews for underwater emergencies.

Ryder. Signaling that he was in position for whatever she needed him to do.

"You know what?" she said to Petrov, her Miami accent sliding into the words as she made her decision. "Fuck your deal."

The combat that followed was brief and violent. Ryder emerged from concealment with the kind of precision that came from naval special forces training, while Miguel and Jin coordinated assault from multiple directions.

Petrov's guards were professional, but they were operating in a confined space against opponents who'd fought their way through international criminal networks for weeks. The outcome was determined by training, motivation, and the kind of desperate courage that came from protecting family.

When the shooting stopped, Petrov was dead, his guards were neutralized, and Zara was cutting her family members free from their restraints.

"Carlos, *mi amor*, you okay?" she asked in Spanish, checking her brother for injuries while he regained consciousness.

"Zara?" he mumbled, confusion evident as he processed his surroundings. "What the hell is going on?"

"Long story," she replied, helping him stand while checking on her cousin Marie. "Right now we need to get out of here."

"Evidence," Jin reminded them, indicating the computer files and documents that represented months of criminal activity.

"Copy everything," Zara decided. "Download the files, photograph the documents, secure whatever we can carry."

The next twenty minutes were controlled chaos as they gathered evidence while preparing for emergency extraction. The cave facility represented a treasure trove of criminal intelligence, but staying too long risked exposure to backup forces that Petrov might have summoned.

"Boat engines," Miguel reported from the cave entrance, monitoring sonar for approaching threats. "Multiple contacts, military configuration, closing fast."

"Viktor's backup," Ryder identified, studying the tactical situation. "Time to go."

The extraction from the cave facility required careful coordination between evidence recovery and family protection. Carlos and Marie were still weak from whatever drugs had kept them unconscious, but they were mobile enough for emergency evacuation.

"Stay close," Zara instructed her family members as they prepared to enter the water. "We're swimming out through underwater caves. Follow my lead and don't panic."

"Swimming through what?" Carlos asked with alarm.

"Trust me," she replied, her federal training and cultural background combining to provide confidence in dangerous circumstances. "I know these waters."

The swim through the cave system was harrowing for her family members, who lacked diving experience and were still recovering from drugged unconsciousness. But Zara's knowledge of Caribbean cave systems and Ryder's naval expertise got everyone through the underwater passages safely.

They emerged from the cave entrance to find the *Siren's Call* waiting with engines running and Tomás coordinating emergency extraction procedures. Behind them, Viktor's backup forces were discovering the aftermath of the assault on their underwater facility.

"Everyone aboard," Ryder commanded, helping Carlos and Marie onto the boat while Zara secured the evidence they'd recovered from Petrov's operation.

"Federal backup?" she asked Tomás as they departed the area at maximum speed.

"Twenty minutes out," he replied, monitoring multiple radio frequencies. "Deputy Director Harrison coordinated real federal response - Coast Guard, Navy, the works."

The reunion with legitimate federal authorities was emotional and complicated. Carlos and Marie required medical attention and debriefing, while the evidence from

Viktor's cave facility needed careful documentation and analysis.

"Your family's safe," Harrison assured Zara as federal medical personnel checked her brother and cousin for lingering effects from their captivity. "We'll arrange protection until Viktor's entire network is dismantled."

"And the evidence?" she asked.

"Comprehensive," Harrison replied with satisfaction. "Between what you recovered from the *Caribbean Star* and what you found in Petrov's facility, we have enough to prosecute criminal networks across multiple countries."

Viktor's reaction to news of his facility's destruction was typically understated.

"Petrov was always too confident," he said with indifference when informed of his operational commander's death. "I suppose this means my associates will need to find new leadership."

"Your associates will be joining you in federal prison," Zara replied firmly. "We got enough evidence to roll up your entire organization."

"Perhaps," Viktor agreed with that dead-eyed smile. "Or perhaps you have simply eliminated one facility in a very large operation. Time will tell."

The Caribbean sunset painted the ocean in shades of gold and crimson as federal forces coordinated evidence recovery and prisoner transfer. Months of investigation had finally resulted in comprehensive victory against international diamond trafficking.

But as Zara watched her family receive medical care while federal agents processed evidence that would put war criminals in prison, she realized the most important victory was personal.

She'd chosen family over federal protocols and somehow managed to serve justice at the same time.

"What happens now?" Ryder asked, standing beside her as they watched the federal operation wind down.

"Now we testify, prosecute criminals, and figure out what comes next," she replied, leaning against his shoulder while federal helicopters transported prisoners and evidence back to civilization.

"Together?" he asked quietly.

"If you want," she said, surprised by how much she hoped he'd say yes.

"I want," he confirmed, his arm tightening around her while the Caribbean night settled over calm waters.

The ocean had kept its secrets long enough. Time to build something new from the truth they'd fought so hard to find.

The federal debriefing process took three days and involved more agencies than Zara had known existed. DEA, FBI, Coast Guard, Navy Intelligence, State Department, and what appeared to be several alphabet soup organizations that wouldn't identify themselves clearly.

But through it all, one thing remained constant - Deputy Director Harrison's commitment to seeing justice done properly, without the corruption that had nearly destroyed the entire investigation.

"The scope of Viktor's network exceeded our worst estimates," he said during a private briefing aboard the Coast Guard cutter that had become their temporary headquarters. "Diamond trafficking, arms dealing, money laundering, political corruption - his organization touched every major criminal enterprise in the Caribbean."

"And now?" Zara asked, studying files that documented the criminal empire they'd helped dismantle.

"Now we prosecute," Harrison replied with satisfaction. "Federal courts, international tribunals, extradition proceedings that will keep prosecutors busy for years."

"What about Martinez?"

"Federal prison, minimum twenty-five years," Harrison said with the kind of finality that suggested plea bargaining wasn't an option. "Her cooperation provided additional intelligence, but corruption at her level demands serious consequences."

The evidence they'd recovered from both the *Caribbean Star* wreck and Viktor's cave facility painted a comprehensive picture of international criminal activity that reached into government agencies across multiple countries. Each document, photograph, and digital file represented another piece of a puzzle that would reshape law enforcement understanding of organized crime.

"Your brother's name will be cleared completely," Harrison assured Ryder during a separate briefing. "The evidence shows definitively that Marcus MacCallum was framed by Martinez's criminal network. Full posthumous vindication, restoration of honors, official apology from the agencies involved."

Ryder's emotional response was carefully controlled, but Zara could see the relief and satisfaction in his green eyes. Six months of grief and anger finally had resolution that would let his brother's children grow up knowing their father had been a hero.

"Thank you," he said simply, the words carrying weight that formal expressions couldn't convey.

"Thank Agent Baptiste," Harrison replied. "Her investigation and your assistance made justice possible."

The personal aftermath was more complicated than the professional resolution. Carlos and Marie recovered from their ordeal with the resilience that came from growing up in a community where people looked out for each other. But the experience had shown them dangers they'd never imagined.

"You really been doing this shit for eight years?" Carlos asked his sister during one of their debriefing sessions. "Fighting international criminals and war criminals?"

"Most of it's boring paperwork," Zara replied, though her recent experiences suggested that statement might need updating. "This case was... unusual."

"Unusual," Marie repeated with dark humor. "That's one way to describe getting kidnapped by Russian arms dealers."

"I'm sorry you got pulled into this," Zara said, guilt evident in her voice. "Federal operations aren't supposed to endanger family members."

"*Mija*, we family," her cousin replied, mixing English and Spanish in the way that felt most natural. "Family protects family, no matter what kind of work we do."

The cultural understanding that family obligations transcended professional duties was something federal training had never addressed. But it was also something that had made her investigation successful where traditional law enforcement had failed.

"So what now?" Carlos asked. "You going back to Miami, back to regular DEA work?"

"I don't know," Zara admitted honestly. "Some things have changed that make regular federal work more complicated."

The main complication was standing at the boat's rail, studying Caribbean charts with the kind of focused attention that suggested he was planning their next adventure. Ryder MacCallum had become more than a mission asset or even a romantic interest - he'd become a partner in ways that federal careers didn't usually accommodate.

"You thinking about staying here?" Marie asked, following her gaze toward the Australian treasure hunter who'd risked everything to help her mission.

"Maybe," Zara said, surprising herself with how appealing the possibility sounded. "Maybe it's time to find out what comes after justice."

The conversation was interrupted by Jin's voice from the communication station.

"Agent Baptiste," she called, "incoming call for you on federal frequency. Deputy Director Harrison wants you in the communication room."

The call turned out to be from FBI Director Sarah Chen, a woman whose reputation for integrity and competence had made her one of the most respected law enforcement officials in the country.

"Agent Baptiste," Director Chen said, her voice carrying authority that made federal agents stand straighter. "Your work on this investigation has been exceptional. I understand you recovered evidence that will reshape our understanding of international criminal organizations."

"Thank you, ma'am," Zara replied, uncertain where the conversation was heading.

"I'm calling because I have an offer," Chen continued. "Joint task force on international organized crime, federal agencies coordinating with international partners, focus on maritime criminal enterprises."

The offer was exactly the kind of career advancement that every federal agent dreamed about. High-profile assignment, international scope, opportunity to make real differences in global law enforcement.

"It sounds like an incredible opportunity," Zara said carefully.

"It is," Chen confirmed. "But it would require full-time commitment, extensive travel, probably years of undercover work in dangerous circumstances."

The kind of assignment that would make personal relationships impossible and family connections complicated. Federal service at its most demanding and rewarding.

"I'll need time to consider the offer," Zara said.

"Of course," Chen replied. "But not too much time. International criminals don't wait for federal agents to make career decisions."

When the call ended, Zara found herself staring at the Caribbean horizon while processing options that would determine the direction of her entire life. Professional advancement versus personal relationships, federal duty versus family connections, justice versus love.

"Sounds like important conversation," Ryder said, joining her at the rail with the kind of casual presence that had become as natural as breathing.

"Job offer," she said simply. "Big one."

"Congratulations," he replied, though something in his voice suggested he understood the implications. "What kind of job?"

"International organized crime task force," she explained. "Years of undercover work, extensive travel, the kind of assignment that defines federal careers."

"And?" he asked, though his weathered face showed he already knew what the 'and' involved.

"And it would make personal relationships almost impossible," she admitted. "Federal service at that level requires complete commitment."

They stood in comfortable silence for a while, watching the sun set over water that had become as familiar as home during their weeks of adventure and danger.

"What do you want to do?" Ryder asked eventually.

"I want to serve justice," she said honestly. "I want to stop criminals who hurt innocent people, want to make sure what happened to your brother doesn't happen to other good people."

"But?"

"But I also want to wake up next to you for the next thirty years," she continued, surprised by her own honesty. "Want to build something together that's bigger than individual careers or missions."

"Those don't have to be mutually exclusive," he pointed out.

"Don't they?" she asked. "Federal agents who take international assignments don't usually maintain treasure hunting boyfriends in the Caribbean."

"Maybe not," he agreed with a slight smile. "But treasure hunters who work with legitimate archaeologists and federal agencies might have more flexibility."

The suggestion carried possibilities she hadn't considered. Ryder's operation was already legitimate, working with museums and following proper archaeological protocols.

Expanding that work to include federal consultation and international cooperation wouldn't be unprecedented.

"You'd be willing to work with federal agencies?" she asked. "Even after what Martinez and the corruption did to your brother?"

"I'd be willing to work with federal agents who care about justice more than bureaucracy," he clarified. "Agents like you."

The next morning brought news that would reshape their decision-making process. Director Chen called back with additional information about the international task force that changed everything.

"Agent Baptiste," she said, "I've been thinking about your unique qualifications and the success of your recent investigation."

"Yes, ma'am?"

"Maritime criminal enterprises require agents with specialized knowledge and unconventional approaches," Chen continued. "Your work with civilian contractors during this investigation suggests possibilities we hadn't previously considered."

"What kind of possibilities?"

"Joint operations with legitimate maritime contractors," Chen explained. "Federal agents working with treasure hunters, archaeologists, and other maritime professionals who operate in international waters."

The concept was innovative and potentially revolutionary - federal law enforcement adapting to criminal networks that operated beyond traditional jurisdiction by partnering with people who lived and worked in those same environments.

"It would be experimental," Chen warned. "No precedent, significant risks, uncertain career progression for everyone involved."

"But legal?" Zara asked.

"Completely legal," Chen confirmed. "Federal agencies contract with civilian specialists all the time. This would simply expand that cooperation to include ongoing maritime operations."

The offer was perfect in ways that traditional federal careers could never be. Serve justice while maintaining personal relationships, work with people she trusted while pursuing criminals who operated beyond conventional law enforcement reach.

"I'm interested," she said without hesitation.

"Good," Chen replied with satisfaction. "Because I've already spoken with Captain MacCallum about providing maritime support for federal operations. He seemed very interested in the arrangement."

After the call ended, Zara found Ryder in the chart room, studying navigation maps with the kind of focused attention that suggested he was already planning their next adventure.

"Federal consulting work," she said, settling beside him at the chart table. "Maritime operations in support of international law enforcement."

"Sounds right up our alley," he replied with a grin that made her pulse quicken. "Fighting criminals, protecting innocent people, working together."

"Together," she repeated, testing the word. "Professional and personal partners."

"Everything," he confirmed, echoing their earlier conversation. "Adventure, justice, love, the whole bloody package."

The federal paperwork took another two days to complete, but eventually they found themselves aboard the *Siren's Call* again, heading toward new coordinates and new adventures as partners in both love and law enforcement.

Viktor was en route to federal prison where he would spend the rest of his life paying for war crimes and international terrorism. Martinez had already been sentenced and would serve her time in a facility that specialized in corrupt federal agents. The diamond trafficking network had been dismantled and its assets forfeited to victim compensation funds.

Justice had been served, families had been protected, and love had found a way to coexist with professional duty.

"What's our first assignment?" Zara asked as they departed Bahamian waters toward wherever federal law enforcement needed maritime expertise.

"Smuggling operation off the Yucatan Peninsula," Ryder replied, consulting the encrypted communication they'd received from Director Chen. "Drugs, weapons, possibly human trafficking."

"Sounds familiar," she said with satisfaction.

"Fair dinkum," he agreed, his Australian accent making the words sound like poetry. "But this time we know who to trust and who's really fighting for justice."

The Caribbean stretched endlessly around them, keeping its secrets while new ones were created. They had each other, they had their crew, and they had meaningful work that served something bigger than individual ambition.

The ocean held all the answers, and they had a lifetime to find them together.

But first, there was one thing that needed to be settled between them.

"Ryder," she said, moving closer to where he stood at the helm.

"Yeah?" he replied, green eyes focusing on her with the kind of attention that made her feel like the most important thing in his world.

"Before we start the next mission," she said, her hands sliding up his chest toward his shoulders, "I think we need to properly celebrate surviving this one."

"What kind of celebration?" he asked, though his darkening eyes suggested he already knew exactly what she had in mind.

"The kind that happens in private," she replied, her body already responding to his nearness. "The kind that reminds us what we're fighting for."

"The crew..." he began, though his hands were already finding her waist.

"Can handle the boat for a few hours," she finished, pulling him toward the main cabin. "Miguel's got watch, Jin's monitoring communications, Tomás knows the course."

"You're sure about this?" he asked, even as he allowed her to lead him below deck.

"Never been more sure of anything in my life," she replied honestly.

The main cabin was quiet and private, afternoon sunlight filtering through the portholes to create patterns of light and shadow on the narrow bunk. After weeks of danger and uncertainty, the prospect of unhurried intimacy felt like the greatest luxury imaginable.

"We did it," Zara said, her hands sliding up his chest as the reality of their success finally sank in. "We saved my family, got Viktor, exposed Martinez, recovered the evidence. We actually fucking did it."

"We did," Ryder agreed, his Australian accent thick with emotion as he pulled her closer. "Your family's safe, Marcus's name is cleared, and the bastards who destroyed people's lives are going to prison."

"And we're alive," she added, suddenly overwhelmed by how close they'd come to losing everything. "Jesus, Ryder, we could have died so many times."

"But we didn't," he said firmly, his hands framing her face with gentle pressure. "We survived, we won, and now we get to figure out what comes next."

"What comes next," she repeated, studying his weathered features in the golden afternoon light. "Together."

"Together," he confirmed, leaning down to capture her lips in a kiss that tasted like salt air and victory and the promise of a future neither of them had dared hope for.

The kiss deepened quickly, weeks of danger and uncertainty giving way to desperate need for connection and affirmation. They were alive, they were together, and they had all the time in the world to celebrate properly.

"I love you," Zara said against his mouth, the words carrying more weight now that they'd both survived everything that had tried to tear them apart. "I love you so much it scares me."

"I love you too," he replied, his hands working at the buttons of her shirt with careful determination. "More than I ever thought possible."

The afternoon sun painted her golden brown skin in warm highlights as her shirt fell away, and Ryder's eyes darkened with desire as he took in the sight of her. Weeks of shared danger had only made her more beautiful to him, strength and courage written in every line of her body.

"You're incredible," he murmured, his mouth finding the sensitive spot where her neck met her shoulder. "So brave, so smart, so fucking beautiful."

"Keep talking like that," she said breathlessly, her hands working at his belt buckle, "and I might start believing you."

"Believe it," he said against her skin, his teeth grazing her collarbone in a way that made her gasp. "Believe all of it."

She pushed his shirt off his shoulders, careful of his healing wound but hungry for the feel of his skin against hers. The contrast of their complexions was striking in the afternoon light - her golden brown against his sun-weathered tan, different backgrounds and experiences creating perfect harmony.

"Your shoulder," she said with concern, noticing the healing scar from his gunshot wound.

"Is fine," he assured her, demonstrating his range of motion. "Antibiotics worked, infection's gone, and I need you more than I need to be careful."

His hands found the clasp of her bra, releasing it with practiced skill and freeing her breasts to the warm cabin air. When his mouth closed over one nipple, she arched against him with a soft moan of pleasure.

"I love the sounds you make," he said appreciatively, his tongue swirling around the sensitive peak. "Love how responsive you are to my touch."

"Only with you," she admitted, her hands tangling in his sandy hair. "You make me feel things I never felt before."

"Good," he said with masculine satisfaction, his mouth moving to lavish attention on her other breast. "Want to be the only man who makes you feel this way."

His hands moved lower, working at the button of her jeans with steady fingers that betrayed none of the urgency she could feel in his kiss. When he slipped his hand inside her panties, she was already wet and ready for him.

"Fuck, you're soaked," he said with appreciation, his fingers stroking through her slick folds. "All this for me?"

"All for you," she confirmed breathlessly, her hips moving against his hand. "Always for you."

He worked her jeans and panties down her legs, leaving her completely naked in the afternoon sunlight that streamed through the cabin portholes. The sight of her golden brown skin, curves and hollows highlighted by natural light, made his cock strain against his remaining clothes.

"Perfect," he said, his eyes dark with desire as they traced every line of her body. "You're absolutely perfect."

"Your turn," she said, reaching for his belt buckle and working it open with urgent fingers. "I want to see all of you."

She pushed his jeans down his hips, freeing his thick cock to the warm cabin air. He was impressive and ready, already leaking pre-cum from the tip, and the sight made heat pool between her thighs.

"I want to taste you," she said, dropping to her knees on the cabin floor and wrapping her hand around his shaft.

"Christ," he groaned as her tongue swirled around the head of his cock, tasting the salt of his arousal. "Your mouth feels incredible."

She took him deeper, using techniques that made him groan and fist his hands in her hair. The sounds of his pleasure encouraged her to be bolder, using her mouth and hands to drive him toward the edge of control.

"Stop," he said suddenly, his voice strained. "If you keep doing that, I'm gonna come, and I want to be inside you when that happens."

She released him with a soft pop, looking up at him with eyes dark with desire. "Then fuck me," she said bluntly, her Miami directness cutting through any pretense. "I need you inside me."

He lifted her easily, settling her on the narrow bunk with careful attention to their positioning in the limited space. When he settled between her thighs, the head of his cock nudging at her entrance, they both groaned at the sensation.

"You ready for me?" he asked, his voice tight with restraint.

"So ready," she confirmed, wrapping her legs around his waist. "I need you, Ryder. I need to feel you filling me."

He pushed inside slowly, stretching her walls around his thickness with careful control despite his obvious urgency.

The sensation was incredible - fullness and pressure and the intimate connection of their bodies joining completely.

"God, you feel amazing," he groaned, bottoming out inside her. "So tight and wet and perfect."

"Move," she demanded, her nails digging into his shoulders. "I need you to move."

He set a steady rhythm, thrusting deep with the kind of controlled power that had her climbing toward climax with embarrassing speed. Each stroke hit her G-spot perfectly, sending waves of pleasure through her system.

"Touch yourself," he commanded, his voice rough with exertion. "I want to watch you come while I'm fucking you."

She slipped her hand between their bodies, fingers finding her clit and rubbing in tight circles. The added stimulation combined with his deep thrusts had her gasping and trembling beneath him.

"That's it," he encouraged, his rhythm becoming more urgent as he watched her face contort with approaching release. "Come for me, love. Let me feel you."

The orgasm built slowly but intensely, pleasure spreading through her body like warm honey until she was crying out his name and clenching around his cock. The sensation of her climax triggered his own, and he buried himself deep inside her as he filled her with his release.

"I love you," he said again as they lay tangled together afterward, breathing hard in the afternoon heat.

"I love you too," she replied, her head resting on his chest while their heartbeats gradually returned to normal. "Think we can make this work? Federal agent and treasure hunter, fighting crime and falling deeper in love?"

"I think we can make anything work," he said with confidence, his arms tightening around her. "We survived

Viktor, Martinez, international criminals, and underwater cave battles. A few federal regulations shouldn't be too challenging."

"Famous last words," she said with a laugh, but she felt the same confidence. They'd fought for justice and won, protected their families and found love, built something together that was stronger than any individual career or mission.

The Caribbean sun was setting as they finally emerged from the cabin, properly dressed and ready to face whatever adventures their new partnership would bring. The crew made no comment about their extended absence, but Jin's knowing smile and Miguel's satisfied nod suggested their relationship wasn't exactly a secret.

"Next coordinates locked in," Tomás announced from the helm. "Yucatan Peninsula, federal consultation on maritime smuggling operations."

"Right then," Ryder said, settling at the navigation console with the kind of focused attention that meant he was already planning their approach. "Time to serve justice and keep the Caribbean safe for honest people."

"Together," Zara added, taking her place beside him as they headed toward new adventures.

The ocean stretched endlessly around them, keeping its secrets while new ones were created. They had each other, they had meaningful work, and they had a lifetime to explore everything the Caribbean waters could offer.

Some partnerships were worth diving deep to find.

CHAPTER NINE

Three days after the destruction of Viktor's cave facility, Zara thought the worst was over. Viktor sat in federal custody aboard a maximum security transport vessel, Martinez was already in federal prison, and the diamond trafficking network had been systematically dismantled by coordinated international law enforcement.

But international criminal organizations didn't die easily, and Viktor's network had resources that federal agencies were still discovering.

"Multiple contacts approaching from northeast," Jin announced from the radar station, her Korean accent sharp with alarm. "Fast boats, military configuration, heading directly for the federal transport."

Zara looked up from the evidence files she'd been reviewing, her federal training immediately alert to new threats. The Coast Guard convoy transporting Viktor to federal prosecution was supposed to be secure, protected by multiple vessels and air support.

"How many?" Ryder asked, moving to study the radar display with naval precision.

"Six boats, maybe more," Jin replied, adjusting her equipment to get clearer readings. "Professional formation, coordinated approach, definitely not recreational traffic."

"Viktor's people," Miguel said with certainty, checking his weapons while studying the approaching contacts through binoculars. "Last play to either rescue him or eliminate him before he can testify."

Deputy Director Harrison's voice crackled over the federal communication frequency, confirming their worst fears.

"All units, we have hostile contacts approaching the prisoner transport," he announced with crisp authority. "Unknown vessels refusing to respond to radio calls, showing hostile intent."

"This is Coast Guard Cutter *Resolute*," came the immediate response. "We have the transport vessel and are prepared to defend against hostile action."

"Negative, *Resolute*," Harrison replied. "These contacts show military-grade equipment and professional tactics. You are authorized to request immediate backup from all available federal assets."

The tactical situation was developing exactly as Viktor had probably planned from his federal cell. Even in custody, the Russian arms dealer was manipulating events to serve his organization's interests.

"He wants to die," Zara realized with sudden clarity. "Viktor knows he's facing life in federal prison for war crimes. His network would rather eliminate him than risk his testimony exposing the entire organization."

"Martyr complex?" Ryder asked, his green eyes studying the approaching threat while his crew prepared for combat.

"Practical calculation," she corrected. "Dead Viktor can't testify against his associates. They eliminate him, destroy the evidence, and disappear into whatever holes international criminals crawl into when things get hot."

"Fair dinkum," he said with grim understanding. "Which means they'll try to sink the entire transport convoy rather than risk capture or testimony."

The federal convoy consisted of three Coast Guard cutters escorting a specialized transport vessel designed for high-value prisoners. Professional setup with proper protocols, but not designed to withstand assault by military-grade weaponry operated by international criminals with nothing to lose.

"Agent Baptiste," Harrison's voice called over the radio, "we need your boat to maintain safe distance from the convoy. This is about to become a combat zone."

"Negative, sir," she replied, making a decision that violated federal protocols but served the cause of justice. "We're the closest thing you have to professional maritime combat support. We're staying."

"Agent Baptiste," Harrison's voice carried sharp concern, "you are not authorized for military engagement with international criminals."

"With respect, sir," she said, her Miami accent thickening as stress brought out her cultural background, "those criminals just made it personal by threatening federal evidence and prisoner testimony."

The *Siren's Call* moved to join the federal convoy despite official protests, Ryder's naval experience and his crew's maritime expertise potentially crucial in the coming battle. They'd fought Viktor's people before and won - they could do it again.

"Contact," Tomás announced from the weather station where he was monitoring multiple frequencies. "Lead hostile vessel is broadcasting demands."

The transmission came through clearly, Russian-accented English that carried the flat professionalism of military contractors operating beyond international law.

"Federal vessels, you are transporting property of our organization," the voice announced with cold authority. "Release the prisoner immediately, or face the consequences of interfering with our operations."

"Property," Miguel repeated with dark humor. "Guess Viktor's people don't think much of his leadership qualities."

"They think enough to kill him rather than let him talk," Zara pointed out. "Which means they're probably more dangerous than Viktor himself."

The federal response was swift and professional.

"Unknown vessels, this is United States Coast Guard conducting lawful prisoner transport," came the authoritative reply. "You are interfering with federal law enforcement operations. Withdraw immediately or face arrest."

"Last warning," the Russian voice replied with ominous finality. "Release our property, or watch your vessels sink in international waters."

The attack began with precision that spoke to military training and professional equipment. The lead hostile vessel fired what looked like military-grade missiles at the federal convoy, forcing evasive maneuvers that tested every aspect of Coast Guard seamanship.

"Jesus fucking Christ," Zara breathed, watching explosions bracket the transport vessel while federal crews coordinated defensive maneuvers. "They really are trying to sink the whole convoy."

"Professional military contractors," Ryder identified, studying the attack pattern with naval expertise. "Ex-military personnel, proper equipment, coordinated assault tactics."

"Can the Coast Guard handle this?" Jin asked, monitoring federal communications while hostile vessels maneuvered for optimal attack positions.

"Not without backup," Ryder said honestly. "Coast Guard cutters are armed for law enforcement, not military combat against professional mercenaries."

As if summoned by his words, new contacts appeared on the radar display - U.S. Navy vessels approaching at high speed with the kind of overwhelming force that suggested serious federal response.

"Cavalry's coming," Miguel observed with satisfaction.

"Question is whether they get here before Viktor's people sink the transport," Zara said, watching the battle develop around the prisoner convoy.

The federal transport vessel was taking damage despite evasive maneuvers, and one of the escort cutters had already been disabled by missile fire. Viktor's people were serious about eliminating their liability, even if it meant killing federal personnel and destroying government vessels.

"We have to do something," Zara said, her federal training refusing to accept watching while criminals attacked law enforcement.

"Like what?" Ryder asked, though his tone suggested he was already calculating tactical options. "We're one boat against six military contractors with heavy weapons."

"We're one boat with superior local knowledge and crew members who've fought these bastards before," she corrected. "Plus, we know how they think."

The plan that formed was desperate and probably suicidal, but it was also their only chance to prevent Viktor's organization from eliminating crucial evidence and federal testimony.

"Ramming attack," Ryder said with the kind of grin that had probably gotten him in trouble during his naval service. "Use our superior maneuverability to disable their lead vessel."

"That's insane," Jin protested.

"Insane is letting war criminals kill federal agents and destroy evidence," Zara replied firmly. "We didn't come this far to watch justice fail because we played it safe."

The attack run required all of Ryder's naval training and local knowledge. The *Siren's Call* approached the hostile formation at maximum speed, using their smaller size and superior maneuverability to avoid missile fire while closing to ramming distance.

"Hold on," Ryder commanded as they approached the lead hostile vessel at ramming speed. "This is gonna hurt."

The collision was tremendous, the *Siren's Call's* reinforced bow slamming into the hostile vessel's side with enough force to breach their hull and disable their weapons systems. The impact threw everyone aboard both boats around like dolls, but it also eliminated the most dangerous threat to the federal convoy.

"Damage report," Ryder called as they backed away from the disabled hostile vessel.

"Hull intact, engines operational, some electronics damaged," Jin reported, checking systems while nursing what looked like a bruised shoulder from the impact.

"Crew?"

"Bruised but functional," Miguel confirmed, helping Tomás secure loose equipment that had been thrown around during the collision.

The ramming attack had eliminated one hostile vessel, but five others remained operational and extremely angry about their tactics. The return fire was immediate and intense, forcing desperate evasive maneuvers through increasingly rough seas.

"Navy backup, ETA?" Zara asked, monitoring federal communications while hostile fire bracketed their position.

"Ten minutes," came Harrison's voice over the radio. "Can you maintain evasive action until then?"

"We'll damn well try," Ryder replied, pushing the engines to maximum power while maneuvering through a maze of missile fire and automatic weapons.

The next ten minutes were some of the longest in Zara's federal career. Hostile vessels pursued them through Caribbean waters that had become a maritime battlefield, while Navy reinforcements raced to arrive before federal personnel were killed by international criminals.

When the U.S. Navy finally arrived, the battle turned decisive within minutes. Professional naval vessels with proper military armament made short work of Viktor's remaining mercenaries, capturing some and sinking others who refused to surrender.

"All hostile vessels neutralized," came the Navy commander's report over federal frequency. "Transport vessel secured, prisoner safe, federal personnel accounted for."

The aftermath was a mixture of relief and exhaustion as federal agencies coordinated evidence recovery and prisoner processing. Viktor's final gambit had failed, his organization was completely dismantled, and the evidence that would send war criminals to prison remained secure.

"Viktor's reaction?" Zara asked Harrison during the post-battle briefing.

"Philosophical," the Deputy Director replied with dry humor. "Apparently he expected his organization to eliminate him rather than risk his testimony. Almost seemed disappointed when the rescue failed."

"Professional criminal," Ryder observed. "Understands the business better than he understands loyalty."

"Either way, he's headed for federal prison where he'll spend the rest of his life paying for war crimes," Harrison said with satisfaction. "And his organization is finished."

The evidence recovery from Viktor's network had exceeded all federal expectations. Document, financial records, communication logs, and digital files that exposed criminal operations across multiple countries and organizations. Each piece of evidence represented justice for victims and prevention of future atrocities.

"What about Martinez?" Zara asked.

"Twenty-five years, no possibility of parole," Harrison replied with finality. "Her cooperation provided additional intelligence, but corruption at her level demands maximum consequences."

The sun was setting over the Caribbean as federal operations wound down and the various agencies began coordinating their returns to normal duties. The *Siren's Call* had been officially commended for her crew's assistance to federal law enforcement, and there was talk of formal recognition for their role in dismantling an international criminal network.

But for Zara, the most important recognition was personal.

"Marcus's name is completely cleared," she told Ryder as they stood at the boat's rail, watching the sunset paint the ocean in shades of gold and crimson. "Full posthumous vindication, restoration of honors, official apology from the agencies involved."

"Thank you," he said simply, the words carrying emotion that formal expressions couldn't convey. "He died believing the world thought he was a criminal. Now his children can grow up knowing their father was a hero."

"He was a hero," Zara confirmed. "And so are you."

The crew was celebrating their victory with Jin's cooking and Tomás's carefully hoarded bottle of Brazilian rum, while Miguel regaled them with increasingly exaggerated versions of their ramming attack on Viktor's vessel.

"Come on," Ryder said, taking her hand and leading her toward the bow of the boat where they could have some privacy. "Time to properly celebrate."

The front of the boat was quiet and private, trade winds carrying the scent of tropical flowers mixed with salt air while the Caribbean night settled around them like a warm blanket. Stars were appearing overhead, brilliant in the clear air far from city lights.

"We did it," she said, leaning against his chest while they watched the stars emerge. "We really fucking did it."

"We did," he agreed, his arms tightening around her. "Stopped the criminals, saved innocent people, cleared

Marcus's name, and kept each other alive through everything they threw at us."

"What happens now?" she asked, though she thought she already knew the answer.

"Now we build something together," he said, turning her in his arms so they were facing each other in the starlight. "Federal consulting, maritime operations, fighting criminals and protecting innocent people."

"And falling deeper in love," she added, surprised by how easily the words came.

"Definitely falling deeper in love," he confirmed, leaning down to capture her lips in a kiss that tasted like victory and salt air and the promise of adventures yet to come.

The kiss deepened quickly, celebration and relief and desire combining to create hunger that had been building throughout the day's battles. They were alive, they had won, and they had all night to celebrate properly.

"I need you," she said against his mouth, her hands already working at the buttons of his shirt. "Need to feel you, need to celebrate what we've built together."

"Here?" he asked, though his hands were already finding the hem of her shirt. "On deck?"

"Right here," she confirmed, pulling his shirt off his shoulders and running her hands over the sun-bronzed chest she'd come to know so well. "Under the stars, on the water, where it all began."

The deck was warm beneath them as they sank down together, clothes disappearing quickly while the Caribbean night provided perfect privacy for their celebration. The boat rocked gently on calm seas while they came together with the desperate hunger of people who'd survived everything that tried to tear them apart.

"I love you," Ryder said as he settled between her thighs, his thick cock nudging at her entrance. "Love your courage, your dedication to justice, the way you make me want to be a better man."

"I love you too," she replied, wrapping her legs around his waist as he pushed inside her slowly. "Love your strength, your loyalty, the way you make me feel safe enough to be vulnerable."

The lovemaking that followed was passionate and triumphant, two people celebrating their survival and success while reaffirming their commitment to each other. The stars overhead and gentle ocean sounds provided the perfect backdrop for their physical and emotional connection.

"Fuck, you feel incredible," he groaned as he established a steady rhythm, each thrust deep and purposeful. "So tight and wet and perfect."

"Harder," she gasped, her nails digging into his shoulders as pleasure built through her system. "I want to feel this tomorrow, want to remember exactly how good you make me feel."

He obliged, increasing the pace and force until she was gasping and trembling beneath him. The combination of their public location and the intensity of their connection had her climbing toward climax with embarrassing speed.

"Touch yourself," he commanded, his voice rough with exertion. "I want to watch you come under the stars."

She slipped her hand between their bodies, fingers finding her clit and rubbing in tight circles while he continued his deep thrusts. The added stimulation was exactly what she needed, and within moments she was crying out his name as her orgasm crashed through her.

"Beautiful," he groaned, his rhythm becoming erratic as her climax triggered his own. "So fucking beautiful when you come."

He buried himself deep inside her as he found his release, filling her with warmth while the Caribbean stars watched their celebration of love and victory.

Afterward, they lay tangled together on the warm deck, breathing hard while their heartbeats gradually returned to normal. The ocean stretched endlessly around them, keeping its secrets while new ones were created.

"Think we can make this work?" she asked eventually, her head resting on his chest while gentle waves lapped against their boat. "Federal agent and treasure hunter, fighting crime and building a life together?"

"I think we can make anything work," he said with confidence, his arms tightening around her. "We've got each other, we've got meaningful work, and we've got the rest of our lives to figure out the details."

"The rest of our lives," she repeated, testing the words. "I like the sound of that."

"So do I," he agreed, pressing a soft kiss to the top of her head. "So do I."

The Caribbean night settled around them like a blessing, warm air and gentle sounds and the promise of adventures yet to come. They'd fought for justice and won, protected their families and found love, built something together that was stronger than any individual challenge.

Tomorrow would bring new missions, new adventures, new opportunities to serve justice while exploring everything the Caribbean waters could offer. But tonight was theirs, to celebrate and plan and dream about the future they'd earned through courage and dedication.

Some partnerships were worth fighting for.

Some love was worth diving deep to find.

And some victories were worth celebrating under the stars.

The morning after their victory celebration brought new possibilities that neither Zara nor Ryder had expected. Director Chen called personally to discuss the expansion of their federal maritime consulting arrangement, and the conversation revealed opportunities that could reshape both their careers and their relationship.

"Agent Baptiste," Chen began with the kind of professional enthusiasm that suggested big developments, "the success of your recent operation has created significant interest at the highest levels of federal law enforcement."

"What kind of interest?" Zara asked, though Ryder's presence beside her at the communication station made even official calls feel more like personal conversations.

"International cooperation," Chen explained. "Caribbean nations, European maritime agencies, Pacific rim law enforcement - everyone wants to understand how civilian maritime contractors can be integrated with federal operations."

The concept was revolutionary in ways that traditional law enforcement had never considered. Instead of federal agents operating alone in hostile environments, they would work with local experts who understood the terrain, culture, and criminal networks.

"What would that look like practically?" Ryder asked, his Australian accent adding international credibility to the conversation.

"Joint operations, shared intelligence, coordinated response to maritime criminal activity," Chen replied. "Federal agents providing law enforcement authority and resources, civilian contractors providing specialized knowledge and capabilities."

"How many operations are we talking about?" Zara asked, trying to understand the scope of what was being offered.

"Initially, six to eight operations per year across the Caribbean and Pacific," Chen said. "Drug trafficking, human smuggling, arms dealing, environmental crimes - any criminal activity that involves international waters and requires specialized maritime expertise."

The proposal was exactly what they'd hoped for - meaningful work that served justice while allowing them to build a life together. Federal law enforcement resources combined with legitimate treasure hunting and maritime expertise, creating something entirely new in the fight against international crime.

"What about support?" Ryder asked with professional thoroughness. "Equipment, backup, legal authority for civilian contractors working with federal agents?"

"Full federal support when operating under our authority," Chen confirmed. "Equipment access, backup coordination, legal protection for contractors working within established parameters."

"And when we're not working federal operations?" Zara asked, thinking about their treasure hunting activities and museum partnerships.

"Complete independence," Chen said immediately. "Your legitimate business operations remain separate from federal consulting work. We're not buying your souls, we're hiring your expertise."

The arrangement was unprecedented and potentially lucrative, but more importantly, it was meaningful work that could make real differences in international law enforcement.

"We're interested," Zara said, meeting Ryder's eyes and seeing her own excitement reflected there.

"Excellent," Chen replied with satisfaction. "Because your first assignment is already waiting."

The briefing that followed revealed the scope of criminal activity that federal agencies were facing in international waters. Drug cartels using submersible vessels, human traffickers exploiting refugee routes, arms dealers operating from international platforms beyond national jurisdiction.

"Environmental crime is becoming particularly serious," Chen explained, showing them satellite imagery of illegal fishing operations and toxic waste dumping. "Criminal organizations are destroying ocean ecosystems for short-term profit."

"That's personal," Ryder said with the kind of quiet anger that suggested direct threat to things he cared about. "My family's been working these waters for generations. Watching criminals destroy marine environments for profit..."

"Exactly why we need people like you," Chen confirmed. "Federal agents can provide law enforcement authority, but we need partners who understand the ocean and care about protecting it."

The first assignment involved illegal fishing operations in the Pacific, massive factory ships operating beyond national jurisdiction while depleting fish stocks and destroying coral reef systems. Criminal organizations with government protection, operating with impunity because no single nation had sufficient resources to stop them.

"Three-month operation," Chen outlined. "Based in Hawaii, working with Pacific rim law enforcement agencies, objective is to identify and prosecute the criminal networks behind illegal fishing operations."

"Hawaii," Zara repeated with interest. "Different ocean, different challenges."

"Same criminal tactics," Ryder observed. "International waters, government corruption, environmental destruction for profit."

"Plus, your crew would be included in the operation," Chen added. "Jin's technical expertise, Miguel's diving capabilities, Tomás's navigation skills - the entire team would be working under federal contract."

The prospect of continuing to work with people who'd become family was appealing beyond the professional advantages. Jin, Miguel, and Tomás had proven themselves under extreme circumstances, and their loyalty and expertise were irreplaceable.

"When do we start?" Zara asked, committed now to a partnership that could reshape international maritime law enforcement.

"Two weeks," Chen replied. "Time to complete your current federal paperwork, coordinate with Pacific agencies, and relocate operations to Hawaii."

"Relocate," Ryder repeated. "Permanently?"

"For the duration of the Pacific assignment," Chen clarified. "After that, you'll have operational flexibility to base yourselves wherever makes sense for ongoing federal consulting work."

The conversation continued for another hour, covering legal authorities, equipment provisions, communication protocols, and coordination procedures with international law enforcement agencies. By the end, they had a comprehensive understanding of what federal maritime consulting would involve.

"This is really happening," Zara said after the call ended, studying the contract documents they'd need to review and sign.

"Federal agents, treasure hunters, and environmental protectors," Ryder said with satisfaction. "Fighting criminals while exploring the world's oceans."

"Together," she added, the word carrying more meaning than any formal contract language.

"Always together," he confirmed, pulling her close for a kiss that tasted like salt air and adventure and the promise of shared tomorrows.

The crew's reaction to the federal consulting opportunity was immediate and enthusiastic. Jin was excited about working with cutting-edge federal technology, Miguel appreciated the opportunity to use his diving skills for environmental protection, and Tomás looked forward to navigating new waters and learning different ocean systems.

"Hawaii," Jin said with obvious pleasure, studying charts of Pacific operations areas. "Completely different diving conditions, new technical challenges, different criminal networks to understand."

"Plus, Hawaiian food," Miguel added with practical enthusiasm. "Always wanted to try authentic Pacific cuisine."

"New waters, new adventures," Tomás agreed, examining navigation charts with professional interest. "Pacific currents and weather patterns, different challenges from Caribbean operations."

The transition from Caribbean-based treasure hunting to international federal consulting required extensive preparation and coordination. Equipment needed upgrading, legal authorities required documentation, and communication systems had to be integrated with federal networks.

But through it all, the most important element remained constant - the partnership between Zara and Ryder that had survived everything international criminals could throw at them.

"You sure about this?" she asked him during one of their planning sessions, studying federal contracts that would reshape both their careers. "Federal consulting work is dangerous, uncertain, potentially career-limiting if things go wrong."

"I'm sure about us," he replied simply. "Everything else is just details."

"Details that could get us killed," she pointed out.

"Details that could let us save lives and protect innocent people," he countered. "Worth the risk if we're doing it together."

The federal paperwork took most of the remaining two weeks, but eventually they found themselves aboard the *Siren's Call* again, heading toward new coordinates and new adventures as officially contracted federal maritime consultants.

Viktor was serving his life sentence in federal prison, already providing intelligence that was dismantling criminal networks across multiple countries. Martinez would spend the next twenty-five years contemplating the consequences of betraying federal law enforcement. The diamond trafficking operation had been completely eliminated, and its assets were being distributed to victim compensation programs.

Justice had been served, families had been protected, and environmental crimes were about to face coordinated international law enforcement response.

"First federal consulting assignment," Zara said as they departed Caribbean waters toward Hawaii and their new Pacific operations base.

"First of many," Ryder replied with confidence, his hand steady on the helm as they headed toward new horizons.

The Pacific stretched endlessly ahead of them, keeping its secrets while offering opportunities for adventure, justice, and environmental protection. They had each other, they had meaningful work, and they had a crew that had become family through shared dangers and victories.

Some partnerships transcended individual careers or missions.

Some love was strong enough to build new kinds of justice.

And some adventures were just beginning.

The ocean held all the answers, and they had a lifetime to explore them together.

But first, there was one more thing that needed to be settled between them before they started their new life in the Pacific.

"Zara," Ryder said, reaching into his pocket as they sailed toward the sunset that painted the Caribbean in shades of gold and promise.

"Yeah?" she replied, studying his expression with growing anticipation.

"Before we start the next chapter of our adventure," he said, pulling out a small velvet box that made her heart race with hope and excitement, "I have a question I need to ask."

The ring was perfect - simple, elegant, with a center stone that caught the sunset light like captured starfire. But more than the jewelry, it was the look in his green eyes that told her everything she needed to know about their future together.

"Zara Baptiste," he said, dropping to one knee on the deck of the boat that had brought them together, "will you marry me?"

The answer came without hesitation, carrying all the love and commitment and hope for shared adventures that had been building between them for weeks.

"Yes," she said, laughing and crying at the same time as he slipped the ring onto her finger. "Yes, yes, absolutely yes."

The Caribbean sunset painted them in golden light as they kissed, sealing promises that would last through whatever adventures the ocean might offer. Behind them, their crew cheered and celebrated, while ahead of them lay Hawaii and new missions and a lifetime of fighting for justice together.

Some partnerships were worth everything.

Some love was stronger than any challenge.

And some horizons were perfect for new beginnings.

CHAPTER TEN

Six months later, Zara stood on the deck of the *Siren's Call* watching the Hawaiian sunrise paint Hanauma Bay in shades of gold and turquoise. The Pacific waters were different from the Caribbean - cleaner, colder, with currents that spoke of distant storms and underwater volcanic activity. But the ocean's power remained the same, and so did the feeling of home she'd found working these waters with the man she loved.

"Morning, beautiful," Ryder's voice carried across the deck, his Australian accent mixing with the sound of gentle waves and tropical birds. Six months of Pacific operations had given him new scars and a deeper tan, but his green eyes still made her pulse quicken every time he looked at her.

"Morning yourself, handsome," she replied, turning from the rail to accept the coffee mug he offered. "Ready for today's dive?"

"Always ready to dive with you," he said, settling beside her to watch the sun climb over Diamond Head. "Especially when we're hunting illegal fishing networks instead of dodging bullets from international arms dealers."

The federal maritime consulting work had exceeded all their expectations. Three successful operations in six months, dismantling criminal networks that had been operating in Pacific waters for years. Drug smuggling operations, human trafficking routes, and illegal fishing fleets that were destroying coral reef systems for short-term profit.

But today's dive was different. Today was their last operation before the wedding, and tonight Zara's family would be arriving from Miami for a week of celebration that would blend Caribbean and Australian traditions into something uniquely their own.

"Jin, what's our status on the illegal fishing surveillance?" Zara called to the Korean woman who was monitoring federal communication equipment while preparing diving gear.

"Target vessel is maintaining position over the protected reef system," Jin replied with technical precision. "Same pattern for three days - fish during federal patrol gaps, disappear when enforcement approaches."

"Classic illegal operation," Miguel observed, checking his underwater camera equipment. "Professional timing, government protection, systematic destruction of marine ecosystems."

The illegal fishing vessel was part of a network that federal agencies had been tracking for months. Factory ships operating beyond national jurisdiction, using bottom trawling techniques that destroyed coral reefs while depleting fish populations. Criminal organizations with enough political protection to operate openly despite international environmental laws.

"Today we get the evidence to shut them down permanently," Ryder said with satisfaction, studying underwater charts that showed the reef system they were protecting. "Federal prosecution, asset forfeiture, probably prison time for the operators."

"And reef restoration funding from the asset seizures," Tomás added from the navigation station. "Turn criminal profits into environmental protection."

The Brazilian navigator had become passionate about ocean conservation during their Pacific operations, learning about coral reef ecosystems and the criminal networks that destroyed them for profit. His weather forecasting skills had proven crucial for timing federal operations around environmental protection priorities.

"Dive plan?" Zara asked, though she already knew the procedure from months of similar operations.

"Standard evidence gathering," Miguel replied, testing his underwater camera systems. "Document the illegal fishing equipment, photograph the reef damage, collect samples for federal prosecution."

"I'll handle federal evidence protocols," she added, checking her waterproof evidence bags and chain-of-custody documentation. "Miguel focuses on environmental damage documentation, Ryder coordinates with federal surface support."

The dive preparation was routine after months of federal consulting work, but the target environment was spectacular. Hanauma Bay's coral reef system was one of the most beautiful in the Pacific, with tropical fish and marine life that made every operation feel like exploring an underwater paradise.

"Federal backup?" Ryder asked, monitoring radio communications with Coast Guard vessels that were coordinating the evidence gathering operation.

"Coast Guard Cutter *Kauai* standing by," came the professional response. "Federal prosecutors are monitoring for immediate arrest warrants based on your evidence."

"Right then," he said with naval authority that had become natural during their federal operations. "Time to nail some bastards who think they can destroy coral reefs for profit."

The water was crystal clear and perfectly warm as they descended toward the reef system where illegal fishing equipment was destroying decades of coral growth. Tropical fish scattered like jewels through the water column, while the reef below showed both natural beauty and criminal damage.

"There," Miguel's voice came through their underwater communication system, pointing toward bottom trawling equipment that was systematically destroying coral formations. "Illegal nets, bottom scraping gear, everything we need for federal prosecution."

The evidence gathering was thorough and professional, months of federal training combining with their natural diving skills to document criminal activity that would result in serious prosecution. Zara handled federal evidence protocols while Miguel photographed environmental damage that would support asset forfeiture and restoration funding.

"Jesus," she said, studying the damage through her diving mask. "They've destroyed maybe ten acres of coral reef for what, a few thousand dollars worth of fish?"

"Criminal mindset," Ryder replied, coordinating their evidence gathering while monitoring for the illegal fishing vessel's return. "Short-term profit, no concern for long-term environmental damage."

The illegal fishing operation was exactly what federal agencies had expected - professional equipment, systematic destruction, and timing that suggested government protection or inside information about enforcement schedules.

"Got everything we need," Miguel announced after forty minutes of underwater documentation. "Federal evidence, environmental damage assessment, probably enough for serious federal prosecution."

"Surface," Ryder decided. "Coast Guard can take over from here."

The ascent through Pacific waters was routine, but the view from the surface was spectacular. Diamond Head rising from tropical vegetation, Honolulu's skyline mixing urban development with natural beauty, and the endless Pacific stretching toward horizons that promised adventure and environmental protection.

"Federal evidence secured," Zara reported to the Coast Guard cutter as they broke the surface. "Ready for arrest warrants and vessel seizure."

"Copy that," came the immediate response. "Federal prosecutors have reviewed your preliminary evidence and authorized immediate action."

The arrest of the illegal fishing vessel was swift and professional, Coast Guard authority backed by federal prosecution that would send environmental criminals to prison while funding reef restoration from seized assets. Justice and environmental protection combined into exactly the kind of meaningful work that made federal consulting worthwhile.

"Three more criminal operations shut down," Jin said with satisfaction as they watched federal agents coordinate prisoner transfer and evidence processing.

"Three more coral reef systems protected," Tomás added, studying his navigation charts with the kind of focus that suggested he was already planning their next environmental protection mission.

"And one more successful federal operation before the wedding," Ryder concluded, settling beside Zara at the boat's rail while federal agencies coordinated the aftermath of their evidence gathering.

The wedding. In three days, Zara Baptiste would become Zara MacCallum, uniting Caribbean and Australian families in a ceremony that would blend federal law enforcement with treasure hunting, environmental protection with international adventure.

"Your family's flight lands this afternoon," she said, checking her phone for flight information while federal operations continued around them.

"Mum's probably driving the flight crew mad with questions about Hawaiian weather and wedding venues," he replied with fond exasperation. "She's been planning this celebration since the moment I called to tell her we were engaged."

"My family's been planning too," Zara said with amusement. "Carlos has been practicing his best man speech for weeks, and my cousin Marie keeps texting me pictures of potential bridesmaid dresses."

The cultural integration had been smoother than either of them expected. Ryder's Australian family embraced Zara's Caribbean background with enthusiasm, while her Miami relatives appreciated his dedication to environmental protection and federal law enforcement support.

"Think they'll all get along?" he asked, though his tone suggested he wasn't really worried.

"They better," she replied with mock sternness. "I'm not having family drama at my wedding."

The afternoon was spent coordinating with federal agencies while preparing for family arrivals. Evidence was processed, reports were filed, and coordination was established for continued Pacific operations after their honeymoon.

"One week break for wedding and honeymoon," Deputy Director Harrison confirmed during their final briefing call. "Then back to environmental protection operations with expanded federal support."

"What kind of expanded support?" Ryder asked, always interested in operational improvements.

"Satellite surveillance, submarine support for deep-water operations, coordination with international environmental agencies," Harrison explained. "Your success has created interest at levels we never expected."

"As long as we maintain operational independence," Zara said, protective of the partnership that had made their federal consulting successful.

"Complete independence when not working federal operations," Harrison confirmed. "We're hiring your expertise, not buying your souls."

The family reunions at Honolulu International Airport were emotional and chaotic in the best possible ways. Zara's parents, siblings, and extended family from Miami's Little Haiti community mixed with Ryder's relatives from Australia's coastal regions, creating a multicultural celebration that spoke to everything they'd built together.

"*Mija*, you look so happy," her mother said in Spanish, embracing her daughter while studying Ryder with the kind of careful attention that mothers reserved for men who wanted to marry their children.

"I am happy, *Mami*," Zara replied, code-switching between English and Spanish in the way that felt most natural. "Happier than I ever thought possible."

"He treats you well?" her father asked in English, his accent thick with protective concern.

"He treats me like a partner," she said honestly. "Equal in everything we do."

"Good," her father decided with finality. "That's how it should be."

Ryder's family was equally enthusiastic but more direct in their Australian way.

"So you're the federal agent who got our boy to settle down," his mother said with approval, embracing Zara with maternal warmth. "We were starting to think he'd spend his whole life sailing around chasing treasure."

"Now he's sailing around chasing criminals and protecting the environment," Zara replied. "Much more respectable."

"Much more dangerous too," his father observed with parental concern.

"We look out for each other," Ryder assured him. "Partners in everything."

The week of wedding preparation was a whirlwind of cultural exchange, family bonding, and coordination between Caribbean and Australian traditions. The ceremony would be held on the beach at sunrise, combining Haitian blessing traditions with Australian maritime customs.

"Beach wedding at sunrise," Marie said with approval, helping Zara with final dress fittings. "Very romantic, very you."

"Ocean ceremony feels right," Zara agreed, studying herself in the mirror while wearing a dress that combined elegant simplicity with practical considerations for beach sand and trade winds.

"Plus, if any international criminals show up to object, you can just dive underwater and swim away," Carlos added with brotherly humor.

"No international criminals at my wedding," she said firmly. "Viktor's in federal prison, Martinez is serving her sentence, and their networks are dismantled."

"What about new criminals?" he persisted.

"New criminals can wait until after the honeymoon," she replied with finality.

The bachelor and bachelorette parties were cultural exchanges disguised as celebration. Ryder's Australian relatives taught the Miami crew about proper beer consumption and maritime drinking songs, while Zara's Caribbean family introduced the Australians to salsa dancing and authentic Haitian cuisine.

"Your family knows how to party," Jin observed with appreciation, watching Uncle Ronny demonstrate traditional fishing techniques to fascinated Australian cousins.

"Your family knows how to drink," Miguel replied with equal admiration, nursing what might have been his tenth beer while Australian uncles shared stories of commercial fishing in shark-infested waters.

"Both families know how to love," Tomás concluded with Brazilian wisdom, watching the cultural exchange create genuine friendships between people who'd never met but shared affection for Zara and Ryder.

The wedding morning dawned clear and perfect, Pacific trade winds carrying the scent of tropical flowers while gentle waves provided natural music for the ceremony. Family members from two continents gathered on the beach as the sun rose over Diamond Head, creating the kind of perfect moment that made everything they'd survived worthwhile.

"Ready?" Carlos asked his sister as they prepared for the processional down the beach toward where Ryder waited with his Australian groomsmen and the Presbyterian minister who would officiate their ceremony.

"Ready," she confirmed, studying the man who stood silhouetted against the sunrise while wearing a simple white dress that felt more elegant than any formal gown.

The walk down the beach felt like floating, family and friends creating a corridor of love and support while the Pacific Ocean provided the perfect backdrop for their vows. Ryder's expression when he saw her approaching made her heart race with joy and anticipation.

"You look incredible," he said as she reached him, his voice carrying emotion that made their families smile with recognition of genuine love.

"You clean up pretty good yourself," she replied, studying the simple white shirt and khaki pants that looked perfectly appropriate for a beach ceremony.

The vows they'd written were personal and specific, referencing their adventures together while promising partnership in whatever challenges the future might bring.

"I promise to be your partner in justice and adventure," she said, her voice carrying across the beach while family members from two cultures listened with appreciation. "To stand beside you when criminals threaten innocent people, to dive with you into whatever depths the ocean requires."

"I promise to be your anchor and your wings," he replied, his Australian accent adding poetry to words that came from his heart. "To support your federal service while building adventures together, to love you through whatever storms the ocean sends our way."

The ring exchange was simple and profound, bands of white gold that caught the sunrise while representing promises that would last through whatever adventures awaited them.

"You may kiss your bride," the minister announced with satisfaction.

The kiss was perfect - gentle and passionate, celebratory and promising, witnessed by family and friends while the Pacific Ocean provided natural blessing for their union.

The reception was held at a beachfront restaurant that specialized in Pacific cuisine, creating fusion dishes that combined Caribbean flavors with Australian ingredients and

Hawaiian preparations. Cultural exchange through food, conversation, and music that made strangers into extended family.

"To Zara and Ryder," Uncle Ronny announced, raising his glass during the toasts, "who proved that love can survive international criminals, federal corruption, and really bad weather."

"To partnership," Ryder's father added, "in work and life and whatever adventures the ocean provides."

"To family," Zara's mother concluded, "that grows stronger by welcoming new members."

The dancing continued until sunset, Caribbean salsa mixing with Australian country music and Hawaiian traditional songs. Cultural celebration that created genuine joy while strengthening bonds between families who'd found common ground in loving Zara and Ryder.

As evening approached, the newlyweds prepared to depart for their honeymoon aboard the *Siren's Call*, a week-long cruise through Pacific waters that would combine relaxation with reconnaissance for future federal operations.

"Time to go," Ryder said, taking his wife's hand as they prepared to leave the reception for their wedding night aboard the boat that had brought them together.

"Time to start the next adventure," she agreed, following him toward the marina where their crew had prepared the *Siren's Call* for honeymoon departure.

The boat was decorated with flowers and white ribbons, transformation from federal consulting vessel to romantic retreat that spoke to Jin's attention to detail and the crew's affection for their captain and his new wife.

"Wedding night suite," Miguel announced with pride, showing them to the main cabin that had been redecorated with white silk and tropical flowers. "Private, romantic, perfect for newlyweds."

"Thank you," Zara said, embracing each crew member with genuine affection. "For everything. The decoration, the support, becoming family."

"You are family," Jin replied simply. "Partners in everything."

The *Siren's Call* departed Honolulu Harbor as the sun set over the Pacific, carrying newlyweds toward private waters where they could begin their married life properly. Behind them, family celebrations continued on shore, while ahead lay a week of honeymoon adventure in some of the most beautiful waters on Earth.

"Mrs. MacCallum," Ryder said as they stood at the bow watching stars appear in the tropical night sky.

"I like the sound of that," she replied, settling into his arms while gentle waves carried them toward their future.

"So do I," he agreed, his voice rough with emotion and desire as they approached the privacy they'd been anticipating all day.

The main cabin was transformed into a romantic sanctuary, white silk and tropical flowers creating intimacy that felt both elegant and perfectly appropriate for their maritime lifestyle. The gentle movement of the boat added rhythm to their movements as they came together as husband and wife.

"I love you, Mrs. MacCallum," Ryder said as they began undressing each other with careful attention that spoke to both desire and the significance of their wedding night.

"I love you too, Mr. MacCallum," she replied, her hands working at his shirt buttons while he traced the line of her jaw with gentle fingers.

The lovemaking that followed was tender and passionate, celebration of their marriage combined with physical desire that had been building throughout the day's ceremonies. They moved together with the familiarity of established lovers and the excitement of newlyweds beginning their life together.

"My wife," he said with wonder as he settled between her thighs, his thick cock nudging at her entrance. "My beautiful, brave, incredible wife."

"My husband," she replied, wrapping her legs around his waist as he pushed inside her slowly. "My partner in everything."

The sensation of their bodies joining completely felt profound and right, physical connection that represented emotional and spiritual union they'd forged through shared adventures and mutual respect.

"Fuck, you feel amazing," he groaned as he established a rhythm that was both gentle and purposeful. "Perfect fit, perfect woman, perfect wife."

"Perfect husband," she gasped, her body already responding to his touch with the kind of immediate arousal that came from knowing exactly how he could make her feel. "Perfect partner, perfect lover."

The rhythm they established was unhurried and deep, wedding night lovemaking that prioritized connection over urgency. Each thrust was deliberate and profound, building pleasure slowly while strengthening the bonds that had made them partners in justice and adventure.

"Touch yourself," he said, his voice rough with desire as he watched her face in the romantic lighting. "I want to feel my wife come around my cock."

The request sent heat straight through her system, and she slipped her hand between their bodies to find her clit. The added stimulation combined with his deep thrusts had her climbing toward climax with steady inevitability.

"That's it," he encouraged, his movements becoming more urgent as he felt her inner walls beginning to flutter around him. "Come for your husband."

The orgasm built slowly but powerfully, pleasure spreading through her body like warm honey until she was gasping his name and clenching around his shaft. The sensation of her climax triggered his own, and he buried himself deep inside her as he filled her with his release.

"I love you," they said simultaneously, the words overlapping as they held each other through the aftershocks of shared pleasure.

"Best wedding night ever," she said eventually, her head resting on his chest while their heartbeats gradually returned to normal.

"Best wedding ever," he agreed, his arms tightening around her. "Best wife ever."

"Best husband ever," she replied, pressing a soft kiss to his collarbone. "Best partner in crime-fighting and ocean adventures."

"Speaking of ocean adventures," he said, reaching for something on the nightstand beside their transformed cabin, "I have a wedding present for you."

The gift was a small box containing diving equipment - custom masks and regulators engraved with their names and wedding date, designed for the kind of professional underwater work that had become their specialty.

"Partnership equipment," she said with delight, studying the elegant engraving that marked the gear as specifically theirs. "For federal consulting and treasure hunting and whatever other underwater adventures we find."

"Forever equipment," he confirmed. "For whatever the ocean sends our way."

The honeymoon week was perfect - diving in waters that ranged from shallow coral gardens to deep-water canyons where whale songs echoed through the blue depths. Federal reconnaissance disguised as romantic exploration, learning Pacific ocean systems while planning future environmental protection operations.

"This could be our base," Zara said during one of their dives, studying an underwater canyon system that would provide perfect cover for federal surveillance operations. "Pacific headquarters for maritime consulting."

"Good diving, strategic location, proper support facilities," Ryder agreed, his voice coming through their underwater communication system as they explored the canyon together. "Plus, Hawaii's not a bad place to call home."

"Home," she repeated, testing the word while they swam through water so clear it felt like flying. "I like the sound of that."

Their return to normal operations after the honeymoon was seamless, federal consulting work that built on their successful environmental protection missions while expanding into new areas of maritime law enforcement. Drug interdiction, human trafficking prevention, illegal fishing enforcement - meaningful work that made real differences in Pacific ocean protection.

"New assignment," Director Chen announced during their first post-honeymoon briefing. "Deep-water mining operations that are destroying seamount ecosystems.

International criminal organization, government protection, environmental damage that could be irreversible."

"Details?" Zara asked, though she was already studying underwater charts that showed mining sites throughout the Pacific.

"Japanese organized crime, Chinese government backing, mining operations that are destroying underwater mountains that took millions of years to develop," Chen explained. "Criminal profits, environmental destruction, and no single nation has authority to stop them."

"Sounds familiar," Ryder observed with the kind of focus that meant he was already planning tactical approaches to the problem.

"Sounds like our kind of work," she agreed, excitement building at the prospect of protecting ocean environments while exposing international criminal operations.

"Six-month operation," Chen continued. "Based in Hawaii but operating throughout the Pacific, objective is to gather evidence for international prosecution while protecting seamount ecosystems."

"Environmental protection and criminal prosecution," Miguel said with satisfaction, studying the technical specifications for deep-water diving operations. "Perfect combination."

"Plus, seamount diving," Jin added with technical enthusiasm. "Completely different from coral reef operations, new challenges and equipment requirements."

"New waters, new adventures," Tomás concluded with navigator's appreciation for unexplored ocean areas.

The briefing continued for another hour, covering legal authorities, international cooperation, equipment requirements, and coordination procedures with Pacific rim law enforcement agencies. By the end, they had a comprehensive understanding of what would become their most ambitious federal consulting operation.

"This is really happening," Zara said as they reviewed operational plans aboard the *Siren's Call* later that evening. "International environmental protection, criminal network prosecution, deep-water operations throughout the Pacific."

"Federal agents, treasure hunters, environmental protectors, and married partners," Ryder said with satisfaction, pulling her close as they watched the Hawaiian sunset paint the ocean in shades of gold and promise. "Everything we dreamed about when we were dodging bullets in the Caribbean."

"Everything and more," she agreed, settling into his arms while considering the challenges and opportunities their new assignment would provide.

The Pacific stretched endlessly around them, keeping its secrets while offering opportunities for adventure, justice, and environmental protection. They had each other, they had meaningful work, and they had a crew that had become family through shared dangers and victories.

Six months after their Caribbean adventure began, they'd built something that transcended individual careers or missions - a partnership that served justice while protecting the ocean environments they both loved.

"Ready for the next adventure, Mrs. MacCallum?" Ryder asked as stars began appearing in the tropical night sky.

"Ready for anything, Mr. MacCallum," she replied, turning in his arms to kiss the man who'd become her partner in everything. "As long as we're diving together."

The ocean held all the answers, and they had a lifetime to find them.

Some love was worth fighting international criminals to protect.

Some partnerships were strong enough to change the world.

And some adventures were just beginning.

But first, there was diving to do, criminals to catch, and coral reefs to protect. The Pacific Ocean was vast and full of secrets, and Agent Zara MacCallum and Captain Ryder MacCallum were exactly the right team to explore them all.

Together.

Forever.

In the deep blue waters that had brought them together and would carry them toward whatever horizons awaited.

THE END

Made in the USA
Coppell, TX
02 October 2025